The
Dismembered

The Dismembered

Jonathan Janz

CEMETERY DANCE PUBLICATIONS

Baltimore

— 2022 —

This is for Brian Keene,
the one who always believed.

Would God I could awaken
For a dream I know not how,
And my soul is sorely shaken
Lest an evil step be taken,—
Lest the dead who is forsaken
May not be happy now.

Edgar Allan Poe
"Bridal Ballad"

Part ONE

Altarbrook

One

J was brooding in my compartment when I first heard Sarah Coyle speak. Had my brain not been so clouded by unhappiness, I might have found the voice dulcet, angelic even. But life had colored my thinking in an unpleasant way, and the only emotion I discerned in the voice from the adjacent boxcar compartment was distress.

I tilted my head to listen.

"...is none of your concern," the young woman was saying.

"When I step out of the car for a bite to eat and find my granddaddy's watch missing," came the response, "it most certainly *is* my concern."

The man's voice was guttural, though not entirely uncultured. I judged the interlocutor a man of early middle age, a laborer perhaps who believed himself above his station and whose perspective was tainted by bitterness and resentment. Further, the man's diction was slightly slurred by drink.

Rage and drunkenness, I thought. *A combustible brew.*

I sat forward, listening.

The woman asked, "Why would I covet your timepiece, sir?" The rustle of clothing, the clink of steel. "I have a perfectly functional one on my person."

Something hungry permeated the man's voice. "Ah, so you do. A bauble like that could fetch twenty quid in London."

My internal alarms began to sound. The man was a scoundrel. I set my book aside—E.A. Poe's *Tales of the Arabesque and Grotesque*—preparatory to rising. I was eager to hear how the young woman would respond.

Her voice was marble-strong, though I detected an undercurrent of fear. "If you come any closer, I'll ring for the porter."

The man chuckled. "You may ring the porter all you like. He's no larger than my sister's lapdog."

I crept to the doorway.

"And what will you do?" the young woman challenged. "Rob me? Pillage my belongings?"

"Now that's a fine idea. I was going to leave it at that Benson watch, but the more I look at you, the more I reckon you can donate to the cause."

"And what cause is that?"

"Keeping your snowy-white ass alive," the man growled.

I stepped around the corner.

The scene I beheld was straight out of a Dickens novel. Hulking thug in heavy brown work clothes towering over a radiant blond woman in a flowing pink afternoon dress. I paused, discomfited not only by the brute's immense girth, but by the young woman's appearance. It wasn't mere beauty that muddied my thoughts; it was her uncanny resemblance to my ex-wife. The supple pink skin, the long, slender neck, and the general air of stubborn independence were all reminiscent of the woman who had humiliated me.

The woman who had caused me to flee Boston.

"What's this?" the brute demanded, favoring me with a countenance as coarse as his voice. Black whiskers coated his jawbone like a dusting of soot. His teeth were as uneven as they were yellow, the eyes as gray and soulless as musket balls. But it was the brow to which my gaze was most compellingly drawn.

The Dismembered

As broad and white as a clipper mast, the forehead twitched and undulated as the man spoke, as though it were a being apart, a dutiful sycophant delighting in its hero's blustering.

"Looks to me," the man said, "like we got ourselves a cockish little wench."

I held my tongue, not yet trusting myself to answer coherently. The contrast between the woman's unnerving beauty and the man's rampant aggression was proving a heady combination.

"You forget something in here?" the brute asked. "Perhaps you dropped your parasol?" He batted his eyelashes.

I glanced at the young woman, who watched me with an expression I couldn't interpret. "It's the funniest thing," I said. "I was just reading a story about a man whose besetting sin was drink. He took to philandering and inhabiting the most decadent haunts imaginable."

"Ah," said the brute with a smirk. "An American. Tell me, is it true you all rut with your horses after a long day of idleness?"

"This narrator," I went on, "he's stewing in 'a den of more than infamy' when he becomes aware of something staring at him from atop a barrel of ale. Do you know what it was?"

"A prancing schoolmaster with twitchy fingers?"

"A cat," I said. "More to the point, an enormous black cat. The narrator takes the animal home, where the man's wife makes of it a household favorite." I uttered a little laugh. "I should mention they already possessed a great many pets. Dogs, birds, even a monkey, an animal of whom I'm sure you're partial, given your own simian heritage."

The man's smirk curdled. "Fancy words. Mayhap you'll have a harder time uttering them if I stave in those girly teeth for you."

I glanced at the young woman, on whose features a dozen emotions swirled. "Is 'girly' lower English slang for 'clean'?" I turned to the hulking man. "In the Poe tale, the narrator becomes obsessed with the destruction of his soul through intentional sin. Drunkenness, debauchery, murder." I fixed him with a meaningful look. "And mistreating women."

All mirth bled from the man's face. "You...impudent... *fucker.*"

I expected the young woman to gasp at the oath, yet she did not, only watched the brute to learn what his next gambit would be.

A haymaker to my face, as it turned out.

Had the blow connected, I would have suffered grievous facial injuries. But due to my heightened state of vigilance, I was able to dodge the blow by dropping to a crouch at the last moment, a position ill-suited for pugilism but sufficient for self-preservation. The brute heaved himself off-balance with the swing, and though I longed to deliver a counterpunch to my attacker's whiskered chin, I knew I stood little chance of success in a conventional sparring match. Brushing aside deep-seated notions of fair play, I reared back and kicked the scoundrel in the side of the kneecap. Despite his prodigious size, the massive fellow buckled as though cleaved by a halberd.

So precipitous was his fall that I scarcely had time to avoid being crushed under him. My lunge and roll carried me into the legs of the young woman, my head, as though to maximize my embarrassment, coming to rest between her feet. I gaped up at her in mortification, yet rather than branding me a lecher, she only regarded me with amusement.

The roar of the fallen brute jarred me back to my senses.

"You miserable whoreson!" the man bellowed. "You shattered my knee!"

I'd half-expected his paws to seize me and eject me bodily from the window of the Pullman, so the sight of him writhing on the floor like a half-squashed bug came as rather a shock. Spittle peppered his lips. His eyelids squeezed together as though to expunge the pain. Obscenities spewed from his mouth, some of them so vile I assumed our lovely compartment mate would

The Dismembered

storm out in protest. But the young woman retained that impish expression, one that suggested it would take much more than indelicate language to make her blanch. I pushed to my feet, wincing at the twinge in my ankle. I must have barked it during the scuffle.

"Would you care to join me next door?" I asked.

Her eyes danced with teasing good humor. "Are you a more refined version of our simian friend?"

"We mustn't assume the worst of others."

"Do you really believe that?"

"As someone who has much reason to take refuge in suspicion...yes, I do."

She watched the countryside rolling past. "I used to feel as you do. Suspicion was my enemy. An impurity from which I should strive to remain untainted."

"And now?"

She gazed up at me. "Now I know such striving is worse than fancy. It's ruinous."

An uncomfortable silence ensued, the only sounds in the boxcar the persistent rattle of the train and the doleful groans of the felled thief.

At length, I performed a slight bow. "Arthur Pearce."

"Sarah Coyle."

I proffered a hand. "Join me?"

Her eyes flicked to the writhing brute. "Are you really a schoolmaster?"

"Hardly. I wouldn't have the patience."

"Wrestler?"

I laughed. "My build is too slight."

"I don't know. Your small waist and broad shoulders would bode well for a wrestling career."

I blinked at her a moment before finding my voice again. "My chosen field is writing, though I'm currently in a state of compulsory retirement."

When informing a new acquaintance of my profession, I was invariably met with one of two reactions. The majority would offer me humoring looks and thinly veiled insults, as though writing stories were tantamount to drunken carousing or a childish game of hide-and-seek. Others with a more inquisitive bent would ask about my current project. Yet seeing as I had not written a word since Angela disgraced me, I was not predisposed to discussing my recent output.

Sarah appeared to note my anxiousness. She said, "I shall accompany you to your compartment on two conditions."

I offered her my hand and helped her rise. "If it is within my abilities, I shall do all I can to satisfy them."

She opened her mouth to speak, then shifted her eyes toward the doorway.

We beheld a grizzled little porter, who studied us with bemusement. His watery eyes alternated between Sarah's fetching form and the sluggishly writhing brute. "Everything acceptable so far, miss?"

"If my being accosted by this cretin is acceptable to you," Sarah answered, "then yes, this journey has begun delightfully."

The porter cringed and seemed to shrink another few inches. "My sincere apologies, miss. I'll return with help so we can get him moved."

I said, "Put in prison, you mean."

The porter stared up at me, appalled. "We don't have the facilities for that, sir."

"I merely meant you can have him guarded until our next stop, at which time a magistrate can be informed—"

"I appreciate Mr. Pearce's desire for justice," Sarah interrupted, "but I prefer to put the unsavory episode behind me." She spoke briskly to the porter. "Do I have your word that this gorilla will leave us alone for the remainder of the trip?"

Relief suffused the porter's face. "Of course, miss."

The Dismembered

"I hope so," she said, "because if you fail to ensure our safety, your company will hear of it. The Earl of Altarbrook has no patience for porters who ignore the wellbeing of their passengers."

The little man paled at this and assured Sarah he would keep the brute away. With that, we moved to my compartment, the porter lugging Sarah's suitcase behind him. We soon found ourselves alone.

I sat across from her. "You were speaking about conditions."

The blazing midafternoon sun firelit her face. I wondered whether she was betrothed. Not that I believed myself worthy of her; downtrodden Americans with dwindling savings and a failed marriage represented poor matches for the beautiful daughters of English nobility.

Perhaps sensing my scrutiny, she sat up a little straighter. "The first condition," she said, "is that you tell me what you're writing."

I must have tightened because she hastened to add, "If we're going to share this space for the next four hours, you're going to speak to me like a friend and not some scandalmongering book critic."

"You're a ruthless negotiator."

"And no lying," she said, boring into me with her cobalt eyes.

I raised my arms in defeat. "What's the second condition?"

She glanced solemnly at her hands, which had begun to grapple with one another. "The second is not so simple."

I crossed my legs, aware that the atmosphere in the cramped compartment had changed. "Go on."

"I'm in my extremity, Mr. Pearce."

"Arthur, please."

"In time," she said. "For now, it shall remain Mr. Pearce. You haven't heard my proposal."

"If it's in my power to—"

"Who can say if it is? My father tells me I'm sanguine by nature, but our current circumstances have robbed me of hope. No matter what direction I turn, I find myself confounded."

Jonathan Janz

I realized with alarm she was on the verge of tears. I sat forward, my hands tingling with the need to comfort her. Decorum, however, prohibited physical contact.

She heaved a tremulous sigh. "My family is one of the oldest in the county. My father, a good man, is a bit whimsical, and I'm afraid he didn't inherit my grandfather's acumen for business."

I withdrew a little. "Your problems are financial in nature?"

If that were the case, I thought, Sarah would find scant succor in me. I barely possessed the means to support my own humble lifestyle, much less rescue a venerable family from fiscal ruin.

"Please listen," she said.

I nodded, vaguely ashamed at the run of my thoughts.

"The money is indeed one aspect of it, but a minor one. We are comfortable, my family and I. We maintain a full staff. The grounds are pristinely manicured, and Altarbrook is in good repair."

"Altarbrook?"

"Our ancestral home, one of the oldest in our corner of England. We possess the financial wherewithal to continue in this fashion for another few years, but failed business ventures and my dissolute brother have ravaged the estate's holdings." She sighed ruefully. "I tell you this not to elicit pity, Mr. Pearce, but to account for my father's eagerness."

"Eagerness?"

She gave a breathless laugh. "Why, to marry off his daughters to wealthy landowners!"

My heart sank a little. "You're being forced to marry?"

"Not me, Mr. Pearce. My younger sister."

I was buoyed by the news that Sarah might yet remain eligible—though I recognized my desire for her as the romantic folly that it was; Sarah would no more consider me than she would the grizzled porter.

"You disapprove of your sister's fiancé?" I ventured.

The Dismembered

Her eyes widened, something almost mad blazing in them. *"Disapprove?* Mr. Pearce, were someone you love in thrall to a monster, you would do considerably more than disapprove."

I could only stare, so taken aback was I at her vehemence. She averted her eyes. "Forgive me. You couldn't have known."

We were quiet a moment before I asked, "What is the suitor's name?"

She looked at me, and her gaze was that of a woman twice her age, one who has seen much of life and was gravely disillusioned by her experiences.

"His name," Sarah said, "is Count Richard Dunning. And the devil himself could not rival his depravity."

Two

The afternoon sun had grown bleaker, the atmosphere in the compartment chillier. As a writer, I appreciated Sarah's sinister description of her sister's ill-chosen suitor, but a strain of skepticism must have shown in my expression.

Sarah sat straighter in her seat. "This is no fairy tale about shiftless drunkards adopting cats, Mr. Pearce. This is dreadful reality."

Chastened, I waited for her to proceed.

"A few months ago, after our accountant's annual visit, I sensed a change in my father. Outwardly he seemed the same merry patriarch, smiling benignly at his guests and doting on his grown children. But I noticed the shadow around his eyes, particularly when he thought no one could observe him."

I thought of my own father, a great man taken from me too early. "A child knows a parent's feelings as well as his own."

She nodded. "My father was terribly distraught, but he claimed all was well. Though I'm not proud of it, I admit to stealing into his office late one night and poring over the documents left by our accountant. I soon understood the shadow enveloping my father." Her lips thinned. "That was less than a fortnight before Count Dunning arrived at Altarbrook inquiring about Violet, my younger sister."

Jonathan Janz

"Why her?"

Sarah's look was darkly humorous. "Is there an answer that will make me sound anything other than the spurned elder sister? The truth is, I don't know why he chose Violet. I have my suspicions, however."

"And they are…?"

"That Violet is more naïve than I or Lizzie."

"You have an older sister?"

"I don't want to talk about her. The Count was polite to the rest of the family, but he fawned on Violet. She only this spring turned eighteen, and Dunning's looks and charm proved too much for her."

"You believe the two events are connected? The dire financial news and Count Dunning's interest?"

"Their close succession is curious, is it not? In any case, the outcome is the same. My Violet plans to wed the Count by month's end, and in doing so, consign herself to a life of degradation."

The word hung in the air. "What, specifically, does she have to fear from her future husband?"

Her gaze was steely. "I refuse to refer to him as that, Mr. Pearce." She pitched a weary sigh. "Everyone regards Dunning with reverence. His estate is greater than any in Western England, his castle the stuff of Gothic novels."

I felt an internal quickening. Gothic literature was an especial interest of mine, particularly the works of M.G. Lewis and Charles Maturin.

"To the simpler intellects in our region, Dunning is a philanthropist, a paragon of landed nobility. A standard bearer for all we hold dear."

"You disagree?"

"He doesn't *age*, Mr. Pearce. I remember encountering him in the village during the summer of my sixth year. He picked a tiger lily and handed it to me. And though a decade-and-a-half

The Dismembered

have passed, he looks the same as he did on that day in the village square."

"Some men age gracefully."

"How many acquire every medical treatise in Europe and dispatch representatives to the corners of the globe in search of occult literature?"

I experienced a stir of misgiving. "Wealthy noblemen can be academically voracious. Eccentric, even. But I hardly believe the accumulation of knowledge proves guilt."

She nodded, unperturbed. "I will tell you a story, Mr. Pearce, and allow you to judge whether my fears are well-founded. I was told this by one of our servants, Tom Erskine. Tom's been head groom at Altarbrook since I was born. I've never seen a man so attuned to the emotions of animals." A fond smile touched her lips. "Tom told me—this was after the Count's second visit— that Richard Dunning was not to be trusted. At that point I was still under Dunning's spell and very much the same little girl who'd been charmed by a tiger lily on the village green.

"'Why ever would you say that, Tom?' I asked. 'Count Dunning is a prince.'"

"'Of witchery,' Tom answered. 'My horses whinny to wake the dead whenever he passes the stables.'"

"I laughed. 'Skittish beasts are hardly a basis for character assassination.'"

"Tom eyed me steadily, his expression so unlike the affable one I'd known my whole life. 'A beast is what Dunning is, Miss Sarah. He kills women in that castle of his.'"

"I stared at Tom, expecting him to make a joke of it. But he didn't smile, nor did he lower his bushy-browed gaze.

"Finally, I said, 'Alright, Tom. Whom has he killed?'"

"Tom looked like he'd tasted something sour. We were near the stables, and the horses were shifting restlessly. As though they comprehended our talk. 'Such stories aren't fit for young ladies such as yourself.'"

"I pretended to pull rank on him, though we both knew I regarded him as an uncle. 'You will tell of these murdered damsels, Mr. Erskine, or I will have your wages garnished.'"

"I thought he would be amused by that, but he just scowled. 'It's not somethin' to tease about, Miss Sarah. It's nasty business.' Speaking heavily, he said, 'One night down at the pub, I was drinking with a mate when a pretty young lass hurries in, drippin' wet from a storm. My mate and I, we hear her ask the proprietor if he knows where she can find Count Dunning's castle.'

"'Before the barkeep can answer, this bloke I hadn't noticed sittin' a few stools down, he stands up and hisses, 'You weren't supposed to mention his name.''

"'The young woman, her mouth works like she doesn't know what to say, and this bloke—one I'd seen drivin' Dunning's carriage around town—he mutters something not fit for polite company, seizes the woman by the arm, and drags her out of the pub.'

"'I stood up to follow them—weren't no cause to treat a lady so roughly—but the barkeep, he seizes me by the arm and tells me it's none of my business.'

"'None of my business?' I growl and march outside to stop the villain from manhandling her. But by that time, the black coach was rattling away. We stayed at the pub several more hours, and I reckon I drank my fill—mind you, it's a rare occasion when I indulge that way, Miss Sarah.'"

"'Of course,' I reassured him. 'Please go on, Tom.'"

"'Well, we was leavin' the pub when we saw somethin' that sobered us up good and proper. 'Twas a woman, Miss Sarah, the same woman we'd seen earlier. She was staggering through the streets, weeping somethin' terrible. It was past midnight by then, and there wasn't no moon to see by, so we couldn't make out why she was carryin' on. But we did see the black coach clattering around the corner and makin' straight for her.'

The Dismembered

"'I started runnin' then, but the ale made me clumsy. I only fell once or twice, but that was enough to allow the coach to beat me to her. Someone in a black cloak swept out of the carriage and lifted her, shrieking, inside.'

"'I didn't credit my eyesight, so I splashed through the street until I reached the site of the abduction. Even though it were spittin' something fierce outside and the light were poor, I could see well enough the swirls of blood on the cobblestones. I knew what I'd seen weren't no trick. And it sure as hell weren't the ale.'"

"'What did you see?' I asked him."

"'Her right hand had been sliced clean off,' Tom answered."

At that moment, the train jostled around a bend. It was only with an effort that I refrained from screaming aloud.

My heart thumping, I said, "You believe your groom's story? Despite his inebriation?"

"I would trust Tom Erskine with my life, Mr. Pearce."

I pondered this. "It's all very disturbing, but I don't see what role I have to play."

She fixed me with a gaze so profound that my legs grew nerveless. Had I been standing, I would have crumpled to the floor like a sack of meal.

"Mr. Pearce," she said, "short of murdering the Count myself, I have exhausted my options for derailing my sister's ill-fated union."

I'm afraid I smiled. "And why would you believe me capable of succeeding where you failed?"

"My reasoning is simple, Mr. Pearce. You are creative and you are brave." She gestured toward her former compartment. "You had no knowledge of me prior to coming to my defense, nor had you history with my boorish antagonist."

"Any man would have come to your aid."

She arched an eyebrow. "You haven't known many men."

"Miss Coyle—"

"You intervened," she said. "Furthermore, you exhibited ingenuity and great powers of interlocution."

"I hardly even know what I said."

"You were marvelous, Mr. Pearce. And though the comparison will do you a disservice, you reminded me of Richard Dunning himself." She leaned forward pleadingly. "None of us can talk to him. I've tried, yet I always find myself deflected, his verbal convolutions on a level far above my own." She slumped against the seat. "No one sees him as I do. That's the most irksome part. It's as though I'm wearing spectacles that render innocuous objects lethal. More than once I've considered the possibility that I'm losing my mind."

"Why haven't you confronted Dunning directly? Forgive my impertinence, but you don't strike me as someone who is easily intimidated."

Something frosty tinctured her manner. "Were I a writer, Mr. Pearce, I might be better equipped to describe the Count for you. He is the quintessential wolf in sheep's clothing. Outwardly, he is a striking figure: handsome, tall, powerfully built. But these characteristics belie his true nature, which is so wicked that demons would shudder in his presence."

Despite the fact that I had never set eyes on the Count, I admit to experiencing a growing antipathy for the man. The image of the weeping woman being dragged into the black carriage recurred in my mind. I imagined the rainswept street, the eddies of blood, and the horror of her severed hand.

"Miss Coyle, you overestimate my abilities. I'm not a hero, nor have I accomplished anything of note in my thirty-two years."

She shook her head imploringly. "Mr. Pearce, I have no other—"

"But I will accompany you to Altarbrook. And if I'm able to thwart the marriage you so fervently wish to prevent, I will."

She favored me with an astonished look. "You would help someone you've just met? I haven't offered you a reward."

The Dismembered

"Serving you will be ample reward."
Sarah grinned warmly, her radiance overwhelming.
If she read the lie in my face, she didn't let on.

Three

As the motorcar conveyed us along the narrow valley road and the sundown shadows stretched, I ruminated on the true reasons for my response to Sarah Coyle's entreaty. My chivalrous tendencies did play a role. From earliest youth I've been captivated by tales of knights and ladies, and I suppose my long-held desire to relive the days of King Arthur had something to do with my decision to choose England for my post-matrimonial healing.

Additionally, my sense of justice was stirred by Sarah's pleas. If Count Dunning were as diabolical as Sarah claimed, the laws of morality compelled me to act. One does not allow an eighteen-year-old girl to be debased by a charismatic man of the world. Nor was it possible to turn my back on Sarah, who had humbled herself by baring her family's financial troubles.

Yes, there were noble motives in my decision to journey to Altarbrook.

But there were others as well.

We said little as the motorcar, a black Talbot Tourer that looked handsome enough but jostled us about on the crumbly road as though we were ingredients in some bartender's concoction, and as we began our passage through even rougher terrain,

Jonathan Janz

I mused about all I had lost when Angela had forsaken me, all I yearned to retrieve in my journey to England.

I had been creatively stunted by the business with Angela. Many are the tales of authors who created poetry out of chaos, whose genius were fueled by domestic tumult. For my part, I write best when my mind is untroubled, when I feel a solid emotional bedrock underfoot. But the situation with Angela destroyed me. Whether the damage was irrevocable, I could not say; all I knew was Boston was spoiled for me, each building, each street, every familiar face I encountered a jeering reminder of my failure as a husband, of my humiliation at the hands of the woman I trusted.

I loathed the emotional miasma in which I found myself. My journey to England, therefore, was about escaping that throttling emotional noose and breathing once again as a capable person, a man of worth and potential. I longed to write a new novel; I was hunting for inspiration. What better fodder for my muse than an intrigue such as the one Sarah had imparted?

I was also searching for distraction. In my profession, the ability to focus one's thoughts is essential. Yet, like an incantation, Angela's condemnations had gained traction in my brain and refused to be silenced.

Had you provided for me, I never would have sought security elsewhere.

You're wearying, Arthur. I deserve a man who can challenge me.

And the worst: *You're no longer the person with whom I fell in love.*

This insinuation, the notion that I had begun a slow decline into inefficacy, pierced me deeper than any other. I pride myself on self-improvement. I admit there exists a strain of vanity in my relentless desire to better myself, but I hardly consider this a mortal sin. I read voraciously each night. I exercise daily, performing calisthenics, going on runs, and lifting heavy weights to harden my muscles. What Sarah had said about my thin

The Dismembered

waist and broad chest had pleased me greatly, for I considered my body a sacred vessel, the only one I would ever be given, and I took pride in honing it.

Yet I am not judgmental of others. My discipline is entirely my own. Unfortunately, no matter what I said to disabuse her of the belief, Angela regarded my devotion to self-improvement a rival and an accusation.

Angela: *Why do you read those wretched books?*

Me: *How can I write well if I don't understand the tradition in which I'm writing?*

Angela: *Reading others can only lead to aping them.*

Me, patiently: *Does a shipbuilder not marvel at a yar schooner? A carpenter at a well-constructed house? How can I miss the opportunity to study a lyrical sentence or a labyrinthine plot?*

Angela: *Shipbuilders and carpenters make respectable incomes. Perhaps you should direct your energies elsewhere.*

"It isn't far now," Sarah said, rescuing me from my miserable ponderings. "Just through the cleft in these hills."

I shifted in my seat, the fog of self-doubt cowling me. *You're not a failure*, I reminded myself. *You haven't reached your summit.*

I clutched my knees, acutely aware of the emotional pressure I was exerting on myself. If I could succeed in helping Sarah, I could lay to rest the fear that Angela was right about me, that I was a farcical figure without skill or prospects. For a moment, the hills looming on either side of us blotted out the westering sun. Then the car disgorged from the shadows, and Altarbrook materialized.

Rarely have I been so thunderstruck.

Sprawling, stunning, Altarbrook married the Italianate and Jacobethan architectural traditions. Three stories around its perimeter, a fourth and fifth story rising from its center, the light beige structure exuded charm and solidity. I couldn't imagine the owner of such a castle struggling with finances, nor could I envision any calamity occurring within those venerable walls.

Sarah was watching my reaction. "What do you think?"

"It's nearly as breathtaking as my host."

Sarah colored at the sentiment.

"Do you mind my confessing that?" I asked.

She glanced at the back of our driver's head, perhaps to gauge whether he was listening. "I haven't felt my best lately. There have been many sleepless nights..."

She looked at me then, and something passed between us. I reflected that misery can bring people together as surely as joy.

Soon we quitted the motorcar and entered the Coyle residence. I could rhapsodize for pages about the intricacies of Altarbrook's interior, the grand foyer with its marbled floor and its vaulted ceilings...

But more interesting to me than the castle's architecture were its people. The first member of the Coyle family we encountered was its patriarch.

Hubert Coyle introduced himself with an ingratiating smile and a grip that, while not overly firm, compensated for its lack of virility with a comforting warmth. He was a graying man of fifty years with a rosy, cherubic face, and a full, though not exceedingly heavy figure. He wore a casual brown suit and carried himself as though Altarbrook were as financially solvent as Biltmore Mansion.

"What a pleasant surprise it is to have an American here at Altarbrook," he said, as though I were an exotic animal from some farflung region.

"I'm grateful for Sarah's invitation," I returned. I gestured toward the soaring ceiling, on which innumerable angels and seraphim danced. "This room is as cheerfully appointed as it is exquisitely designed."

He beamed, taking in the view as if for the first time. "It is, isn't it? I often give thanks that my ancestors commissioned such skilled artists."

The Dismembered

"Altarbrook has been in your family from the beginning?"

He nodded. "The First Earl of Altarbrook was a shrewd businessman. He bought up the surrounding area when prices were low and parlayed his investments into the construction of this house. Generations of Coyles owe a debt to his foresight."

At this, a hint of melancholy darkened his brow, but it was so subtle that I might not have noticed it had I not been aware of the family's financial downturn. He and Sarah led me into a capacious parlor, where a young man reclined on an olive-hued brocade sofa. There were many paintings adorning the walls, and one in particular caught my eye. The portrait hung above the hearth, and the woman it featured appeared as graceful as she did benevolent. Not the sort of face that enkindled lust exactly, but rather a visage one could love and cherish.

"Fetching, isn't she?" Hubert said at my side.

"Who is it?"

"A distant ancestor," he answered. "Charlotte was her name, I believe."

I nodded, my gaze drifting toward the mantle, on which were displayed a trio of pistols.

"Ah, yes," Hubert said, nodding at them. "I used to be quite a marksman."

"Were you in the war?" I asked, referring to the bloody Boer conflict.

"Briefly," he said, a shadow passing over his face. "I enlisted, but I never saw real battle."

"Father wishes he had better stories to tell," the young man on the sofa said.

"It isn't that," Hubert answered, his frown deepening. "It's what I learned of the war afterward. Had I known how we were treating the women and children of our adversaries, I never would have joined the effort." He regarded the Oriental rug beneath us as if replaying a string of terrible memories.

I said, "War is rarely a humane business."

Jonathan Janz

"Quite right, Mr. Pearce. Quite right." Hubert shook himself free from whatever dark mental realm he had entered. "Good day, Jimmy," he said, smiling broadly. "Come say hello to our guest."

The young man rolled his head slowly in our direction and eyed us without interest.

"Put down your absinthe and get off the couch, is what father means," Sarah said.

Hubert's expression grew strained. "Jimmy is my son and Sarah's older brother, though you'd never guess it by the way she speaks to him."

"I have no patience for wastrels," Sarah explained. "Especially ones with whom I have the bad fortune to be related."

"At any rate," Hubert hurried on, "I'm training Jimmy in the running of the estate, and he's catching on swimmingly."

"When he's sober," Sarah muttered.

Jimmy's mouth opened in a lazy grin. "Dear Sarah. Have you latched onto another unsuspecting bachelor in an attempt to fend off spinsterhood? He looks a bit tattered around the edges."

Sarah gave him a freezing look and seemed about to respond when Hubert interceded. "Are you a reader, Mr. Pearce?"

"Yes, I am," I answered. "As a matter of fact, I'm a writer."

Hubert's face spread into a look of rapture. "Ah, that's splendid! Altarbrook boasts one of the finest libraries in the country. Would you care to see it?"

"I'd be honored, Mr. Coyle."

He clapped me on the shoulder. "Hubert, please. We don't rest on formality here."

"Then if it's no trouble, I shall simply be Arthur," I returned. "Mr. Pearce makes me think of my father, and though a great man, he has been gone these fifteen years."

Jimmy barked out a harsh laugh. I spun in his direction, forgetting for a moment my role as polite houseguest. "Did I say something amusing?"

The Dismembered

Jimmy tilted his glass of absinthe, swallowed, and gazed upon me with a look of infuriating derision. "Everything you say is amusing," he said in a high drawl. "You shall be a welcome diversion to our monotonous march toward obscurity."

Sarah stiffened. "You indolent bastard."

"Sarah!" her father said. "Can't you and your brother cease bickering for a single night?" He turned to me. "You'd think after all these years they could find some common ground."

Sarah's upper lip curled. "He wallows in mud, Father. I have no desire to stand here while he slings it at us."

Jimmy brayed laughter and spilled absinthe on the sofa.

Hubert shuttled us down a short hallway toward a ten-panel mahogany door. "Do you enjoy the classics, Arthur?"

"I enjoy anything well-written, though I have a particular admiration for the works of Edgar Allan Poe."

Hubert shook his head as he reached for the doorknob. "I've never read him."

Sarah made no comment. Judging from her expression, she was still fuming from her verbal scuffle with Jimmy.

Hubert opened the door and flourished a hand. "Our collection is at your disposal."

I have visited libraries in Boston, New York, and Philadelphia. I have browsed the shelves of some of the most expansive book repositories in the western hemisphere.

The library at Altarbrook surpassed them all.

It wasn't the size of the room that awed me. The space was roughly sixty-by-eighty feet, a simple rectangle in design, though numerous alcoves and bay windows imbued the room with character. The coffered ceiling was of stamped bronze, but rather than casting the library into a state of gloom, the rich metal imparted a sense of warmth and sanctuary. The castle had been equipped with electricity, and the library benefited enormously from the many wall and table lamps that cast motes of light onto various reading areas. A crystal chandelier also spread luminance over the library's center, and it was toward this glow that I ventured.

Some of Sarah's good humor returned. "Do you like it?"

"It's spectacular," I murmured.

"Who's the drummer?" a voice asked.

Hubert gasped; Sarah and I whirled to face the speaker.

A woman in a black evening gown reclined in a window seat. Outlined by the darkening sky and gilded by a nearby table lamp, her lengthy blond hair glinted like spun gold. The languidness of her gaze elicited a powerful lurch in my stomach. Unlike Sarah's face, this woman's expression suggested I was some unsavory genus of insect, one that sullied the castle with my presence.

"My heavens, Lizzie! You gave us a scare." A hand on his heart, Hubert gestured toward the woman occupying the window seat. "Arthur, this is my eldest daughter Elizabeth." He smiled at her fondly. "I should have known you were in here."

Sarah said, "Better than interacting with real people, eh Lizzie?"

Lizzie eyed me. "What are you selling? Washboards? Salad bowls? Trousers with frayed cuffs?"

I frowned at the bottoms of my pant legs, which were indeed a bit threadbare.

"Such graciousness," Sarah said.

Hubert pushed on gamely, refusing to acknowledge the enmity between his daughters. "My Lizzie is a fanatic on literature. I've often considered renaming the library the Elizabeth Room."

"Mr. Pearce is not a salesman," Sarah said, chips of ice flaking from her words. "He's an author."

"What do you write?" Lizzie asked.

Hubert clapped a palm to his forehead. "I didn't think to ask. What sort of subject matter do you favor, Arthur?"

I regarded my shoes, which seemed plain and lusterless in

these opulent surroundings. "I suppose you would call it the literature of the fantastic."

"Ah," said Hubert, though I could tell he had no idea what to make of my description.

Sarah was watching me curiously, but it was Lizzie who asked, "Is it bloody?"

I refused to wither under her gaze. "When the situation demands it."

Hubert frowned. "Oh, I do hope it isn't gratuitous. When I crack open a book I have no desire to visit the Grand Guignol."

I approached Lizzie. Her eyes were a deep azure, the irises spangled with greens and yellows. "What are you reading?"

"LeFanu," she answered. "A tale of gratuitous lust."

Hubert uttered a grunt of wounded propriety, but Sarah's tone remained flat. "Why bother reading about it, Lizzie? You've plenty of firsthand knowledge."

I expected Lizzie to hurl invective at her younger sister. Instead, she raised a knee and laced her fingers around it. In doing so her black dress slithered open, revealing a sinuous thigh. "Mr. Pearce appears to appreciate the female form, Sarah. I wonder if he could teach you a thing or two."

I'm sure I blushed furiously, but Sarah only glowered at her older sister. "Come, Arthur. You've had a long journey, and you deserve a comfortable room and a warm meal."

Lizzie's gaze mocked me. "Yes, Mr. Pearce. Why don't you make yourself comfortable. We wouldn't want to let a stranger visit without putting on a show."

Four

My sleeping quarters were twice the size of my entire Boston apartment. The adjoining washroom was equipped not only with toilet, sink, and a gigantic clawfoot tub, it also contained a bidet, an invention I'd read about but had never encountered. I must admit to feeling a bit scandalized by the rush of icy water against my nether regions.

I was toweling myself off and scowling at the bidet when I heard the baying of hounds. Buttoning my trousers and rushing to the window, I scanned the semidark grounds for the source of the cacophony. Though the early October sky was enameled in the purple of funeral flowers, as I squinted through the windowpane I was able to make out a series of outbuildings I hadn't noticed earlier. Positioned as I was in the rear of the castle, I could discern the stables, a hostelry, and what was undoubtedly a tack room. Behind those, just visible from my vantage point, was a low-walled pen containing a trio of large, snapping dogs. Their fur was sable, their shoulders rippling with vitality. Their ivory fangs and the whites of their eyes flashed as they barked and growled.

An older man came into view wearing simple clothes, a brown wool cap, and sporting a knobby walking stick. A burlap sack clutched to his side, the man limped into the midst of the hellhounds without fear. The hounds crouched at his feet, their hides bristling and their lips undulating in perpetual snarls. I cursed the immovability of the bathroom window, for I wished to hear with greater clarity what the man said to the dogs.

The burlap sack began to writhe.

Fascinated, I hurried from the bathroom to the bedroom and cranked open a casement window, cringing a little at the way it screeched. I'm not certain why I wanted to avoid detection, but for reasons I couldn't explain, I yearned to remain hidden from the man's view.

The dogs vibrated with eagerness, harsh growls rumbling in their throats.

"Easy there, children," the man soothed. "Easy does it."

One hound lunged at the writhing sack, and the man leveled an admonitory finger. "You just keep your britches on, Molly, or you'll be watchin' your brothers eat."

Molly, who was every bit as huge and ferocious-looking as her brothers, uttered a sulky growl but didn't snap again.

"There now," the man said, untying the top of the sack. The animals' growls intensified, their eyes widening maniacally. The burlap sack was positively dancing in the man's hand. He reached inside and lifted out an animal. I expected a large hare or perhaps a barnyard pest, a fox or a weasel.

I didn't expect a cat.

Here I must make a confession. In speaking to the brute in the boxcar earlier that day I had made light of the Poe tale I had been re-reading, the notorious shocker "The Black Cat." In truth, I find the narrator's mistreatment of the cat unconscionable. On many occasion I have seen dogs kicked by mean-spirited owners, have heard of cats being drowned by city officials striving to keep the feline population in check.

Yet nothing could prepare me for what I witnessed in that gloomy kennel.

The Dismembered

The man had buried his fingers in the cat's voluminous neck fur. The animal in his clutches, I saw, was of the long-haired variety, dark gray with splotches of black and white, with a body that, while not overlarge, had not missed many feedings.

When it beheld the snapping dogs, the cat began to yowl.

The man laughed heartily, his belly jiggling. "Want some of this pussy, do you?"

I frowned, half at the man's vulgarity, half at the jolly way he was carrying on. I knew that animals needed sustenance, but did the provision of food have to take on such a macabre bent? This seemed more like a ritualistic slaughter than a twilit meal.

One of Molly's brothers darted. The shrill cry the cat emitted set my teeth on edge. I squinted into the gloom to see why the cat's cries had altered so, for the man still clutched it by the neck. Then I saw the dogs swarming over one another in a frenzy to get at some prized object, and I realized that the leaping dog had bitten off one of the cat's hind paws.

The cat squirmed helplessly in the man's grip as the hounds battled for the severed paw. Finally, one of the hounds—Molly, I guessed—made away with it, which only augmented her brothers' eagerness to procure a choice morsel of their own. One of the dogs hurtled at the cat's exposed belly, and in a flurry of claws, tore open the poor animal's stomach.

I turned away, sickened, but not quickly enough. I had seen the snarling canines unzipping the squalling cat's belly, had glimpsed the entrails stringing out of its spraying abdomen. And yet the man's voice continued to goad the hounds, the merry laughter like pitchfork tines to my ears: "That's a lovely bit there, Tarsus! Come now, Petey, chew your food. There you are…gobble it down…"

Without realizing it, I had clamped my palms over my ears in an effort to escape the hideous scene, and though this muffled the man's abhorrent encouragement, my curiosity compelled me to risk one last glance out the window.

Would that I hadn't looked!

For what I saw made me hate the man to an even greater degree. Rather than casting the dying animal into the hounds' midst and bringing an end to this depraved ritual, the man continued to raise and lower the weakly thrashing feline in an effort to further incite his dogs. The scene in the stone-walled kennel no longer resembled a nightly feeding, but a Bosch painting come to life. The eviscerated animal waved its forepaws in futile resistance. The growling hellhounds leaped at their helpless prey, ripping scraps of fur and tissue from the animal and drenching their coats in the crimson gush.

Blood had spattered the man's cheeks and forehead, so that he reminded me of an overzealous butcher taking an unhealthy pleasure in his work. Yet a butcher served a purpose, fulfilled a necessary function in the machinery of society. This man was a ghoul. Like the narrator in the Poe tale, here was an individual whose atrocities stemmed from a desire to inflict pain, to destroy innocence, to perform the devil's handiwork and pervert whatever nobility resided in man's breast. His laughter taunted me, made my head swim with heartache and nausea.

I cranked shut the casement window and stood panting in the gloom.

Though I was expected downstairs, I couldn't imagine mustering a proper appetite. A thought was nagging at me, and though I attempted to dismiss it as fancy, it refused to be dislodged.

Was the man I'd watched torturing that poor cat the same Tom Erskine whom Sarah held in such high esteem? He couldn't be, else Sarah's judgment was far less astute than I had believed. More likely the man was another of the family's employees. Since Erskine was head groom, the fiend might be under Erskine's supervision, and if Erskine were as good-hearted

The Dismembered

as Sarah claimed, he'd no doubt want to be apprised of such ghastly behavior from one of his underlings.

Try as I might, I could not rid my mind of the memory of that poor cat. The animal's death yowls still rang in my ears.

Sick at heart, my stomach roiling, I commenced getting dressed.

Five

The cries of the doomed cat fresh in my ears, I fled my sleeping quarters and entered the wainscoted dining room. Dinner was served for seven, though only three places at the pallid wooden table were occupied. Seated at the head, his wife and Sarah flanking him, Hubert bade me sit and noticed me inspecting the table's surface.

"It's larch," Hubert said. "Toughest stuff in the world. We had it made to replace its predecessor because of its water resistance."

Mrs. Coyle—tall, slender to the point of emaciation, and as dark-haired as her son—said, "Jimmy always spilled his drink as a toddler."

"He spills his drink as an adult," Sarah said under her breath.

Mrs. Coyle didn't appear to register the insult. "Where is Jimmy tonight? I had Mrs. Bramlage prepare a roast for him."

Sarah speared a cucumber slice, brought it to her mouth. "Jimmy is drinking his dinner."

This time Mrs. Coyle's disregard of her daughter's belligerence was more pointed. She nodded toward a purple vase. "The hyacinths look lovely, don't you think, Hubert?"

"Lovely," Hubert agreed, though he didn't look up from his salad.

Mrs. Coyle directed an exaggerated smile at her daughter. "How was London, dear?"

"Tolerable. The ride home was better."

My face burned with pleasure.

Mrs. Coyle regarded me over her glass of Cabernet. "Mr. Pearce does seem an intriguing gentleman. I don't blame you for inviting him."

Sarah glanced at me warmly. "Arthur is working on a new novel, Mother."

"That's wonderful!" Mrs. Coyle exclaimed. "I *so* respect a man of learning. Take our friend Richard Dunning. He possesses an absolutely insatiable craving for knowledge." She sipped her wine. "I thought our library at Altarbrook was impressive until I heard about Magnus."

"Magnus?" I asked.

"Castle Magnus," Hubert explained. "The home of Violet's fiancé."

There was a thick silence. I chanced a look at Sarah, who was glaring at her salad as though it had wronged her.

"Richard has the most eclectic taste," Mrs. Coyle went on. "When he isn't donating money to the orphanage or presiding over one council or another, he is reading. Violet claims he spends half the day lost in books."

I sampled my Cabernet. "What exactly is his area of study?"

Sarah said nothing, but I could see from her tense posture that she was listening closely, perhaps hoping her mother would let slip some damning detail.

Mrs. Coyle swallowed a sizeable quantity of wine. "Oh, you'd have to ask Violet about that. We don't concern ourselves with Richard's academic pursuits."

"Perhaps," I ventured, "Count Dunning's pursuits are more than academic."

The Dismembered

Mrs. Coyle's expression went blank. "Whatever do you mean?"

Sarah's eyes burned into me. I reminded myself it was to her I owed my allegiance. It would be unfortunate to alienate Mrs. Coyle, but if Sarah viewed me as her champion, I would happily accept the tradeoff.

I broke off a hunk of rye bread. "I respect learnedness as much as anyone. After all," I said, buttering my bread, "writing fiction requires the study of *everything*, from the arcane lore of the ancients to the latest advances in manpowered flight."

Hubert appeared pleased. "Well said, Arthur." He gave Sarah an approving look.

I went on, emboldened. "And while an understanding of these topics possesses value independent of any application, it is the desire to utilize this knowledge that lends passion to its absorption. Is there anyone who studies the vicissitudes of the Wright Brothers more passionately than the aviator whose very life might depend on the safety measures pioneered at Kitty Hawk?"

Mrs. Coyle frowned. "Surely you aren't claiming Richard's studies are meant to prevent his destruction?"

"The avoidance of catastrophe is only one possible motive, Mrs. Coyle. There are others equally likely."

"Such as?"

"Perhaps Mr. Dunning hopes to gain something he lacks."

She smiled incredulously. "And what on earth could a man such as Richard Dunning need?"

"A precious object perhaps. Something he once possessed but does no longer."

Mrs. Coyle's expression grew more puzzled. "Richard is one the wealthiest men in Europe. If tales are true, his castle is a riot of opulence. Therefore, I must put the question to you again, Mr. Pearce: What could such a man lack?"

"A soul?" Sarah asked, and her mother shot her a freezing look.

Jonathan Janz

"Singlemindedness is not the same as soullessness," I said. "I have never met Mr. Dunning, but if all Sarah says is true, it could be that his pursuit of young Violet is another instance of his obsessiveness." I turned to Hubert. "Sarah tells me that Violet's relationship with Mr. Dunning has advanced with uncanny swiftness."

Hubert shrugged. "Not every courtship needs to drag on like a lame nag."

"No doubt true," I allowed. "But I wonder…in the case of young Violet…a situation in which the age difference is so pronounced and the families involved so vital to the welfare of the county—"

A voice spoke from my right. "I see you've poisoned another gullible soul against my true love."

A young woman who could only be Violet Coyle glowered at us from the doorway. Garbed in a light blue dress, her hands sheathed in white gloves, and her golden hair curled into ringlets, Violet looked far too young to be engaged to anyone, let alone a man at least a decade my senior. Unlike Sarah, whose body had developed voluptuously in the places to which a man's eye is drawn, Violet retained the willowy thinness of adolescence. Add to that her ringlets and childlike features, and it was with difficulty that I could believe her age to be the stated eighteen years.

Defiantly, she strode into the dining room and fixed me with a singularly baleful stare. "I suppose she's told you of Richard's bizarre rituals and his devil worship."

I met her iciness with good humor. "The only devil we've discussed is the lout we encountered on the train from London."

Hubert leaped on the topic. "Sarah tells me you were marvelous, Arthur." He glanced at his wife, gestured toward me with a cherry tomato impaled on a fork. "It was providence that brought Mr. Pearce and our Sarah together."

Violet's voice was guarded. "Your name is Pearce?"

The Dismembered

Sarah shot a glance at her sister. Something seemed to pass between them, but before I could unravel its import, Mrs. Coyle looked at me with renewed interest. "You confronted this villain?"

"A thief," Hubert put in.

Mrs. Coyle's eyes glittered. "Do share the details, Mr. Pearce."

Given her enthusiasm, I could only comply. As Violet sat to dinner—keeping as far away from Sarah as possible, I noted—I related the incident, doing my best to embellish Sarah's role while diminishing my own. The alteration of the tale had the desired effect, for Sarah abandoned her silent warfare with her sister and amended my account to such a degree that to her mother I must have seemed an Arthurian knight reincarnated.

Mrs. Coyle leaned toward me with a smile that was almost flirtatious. "And for how long do we have the honor of entertaining the brave Mr. Pearce?"

I dabbed my mouth with the napkin. "Mrs. Coyle, I—"

"Indefinitely," Sarah said.

I raised my eyebrows at her, and the avidity of her gaze caused my stomach to perform a giddy somersault.

"That's *splendid*," Hubert declared. "We'd be honored if you'd extend your visit."

Sarah regarded her younger sister. "What about tomorrow morning, Violet?"

Violet favored Sarah with a thin-lipped smile. "What of it?"

"Might your beloved lord and master allow another guest for luncheon?"

"My Richard," Violet said, enunciating each consonant, "is renowned for his hospitality."

Mrs. Coyle clasped her hands. "Oh, this is divine. Count Dunning has prepared for us a tour of Castle Magnus."

I favored Hubert with a sidelong glance. "You've never been there before?"

Hubert seemed about to respond when Mrs. Coyle cut in. "No one in the family has set foot there, save dear Violet, of course."

"Odd," I muttered.

Violet tilted her head, her unseamed brow darkening. "You disapprove of my fiancé's reclusiveness, Mr. Pearce?"

"It's not disapproval I meant to convey. Merely surprise. After all, you are to be married…"

"In a week," Sarah supplied.

"…and your parents haven't been given the chance to inspect their youngest daughter's new habitation?" I shrugged. "It struck me as strange, that's all. But I know you English do things differently."

Sarah turned a triumphant gaze on her parents, who exchanged a glance of worries confirmed.

Violet's body went ramrod straight. "Richard is too devoted to his work to throw weekly soirees."

I raised my Cabernet. "I hope his devotion to you is equally ardent."

If a look could do injury, the stare Violet directed at me would have sent me to the infirmary. "Our guest is impertinent." She crumpled her napkin and cast it aside. "I shall retire for the night."

Hubert looked stricken, and Mrs. Coyle said something to assuage her daughter. But Sarah regarded me with a look of such adoration that I wondered whether I might steal a kiss from her by the end of my stay at Altarbrook.

When Violet had gone, the servants arrived with the roast and an embarrassment of side dishes. My appetite restored, I ate greedily, and soon, edified by another bottle of Cabernet, Mr. and Mrs. Coyle were laughing and regaling me with stories of Sarah's childhood, stories by which she pretended to be embarrassed but, I sensed, was secretly pleased to hear retold in my presence. The affection between her and her father, particularly, was marvelous to behold, and it made me regret the loss

The Dismembered

of my own dad, who, while not as convivial as Hubert Coyle, had been equally brimming with paternal love. It was nearing nine o'clock when dinner ended. Sarah volunteered to escort me to my room.

"Ordinarily," she said, "we would retire to the parlor for drinks and more of father's mortifying tales about me—"

"Which were fascinating, by the way."

"However," she continued, smiling, "tomorrow's visit to Castle Magnus is of grave import, and I'm sure Mother and Father don't want to arrive at the Count's estate with headaches and upset stomachs."

We made our way down the second story corridor, my gaze marking the rich tapestries. "How are you feeling about tomorrow's appointment?"

"Before today, I felt nothing but vexation and a confounding sense of impotence." She glanced up at me, and my insides gave a pleasant lurch. "But after seeing the way you handled my family, I find myself clinging to a vestige of hope, no matter how scant."

"Sarah," I said as we reached my door. "You shouldn't place disproportionate faith in me. I haven't laid eyes on the Count. What if I find him as charming as your parents do? What if the match proves a sound one?"

"It isn't," she said. "My sister sees in Richard Dunning what he wishes her to see, namely a tall, robust nobleman with a brilliant mind. Like the rest of the county she is bewitched by his charm."

"You make him out like some hero in a medieval romance."

"To the undiscerning, he's exactly that." A sultriness deepened her voice. "But not to me."

My throat grew thick. "No?"

She stepped closer, the electric wall sconce bright enough to limn her features in a warm coral glow. "A hero is savvy enough to form his own judgments, to make his way in the world."

Jonathan Janz

Her eyes slid down my body and returned to lock with mine. "Someone who will fight for the woman he esteems."

I was incapable of coherent thought, much less eloquent speech.

Sarah placed her hands on my chest, leaned up, and kissed me softly on the cheek. When her heels again met carpet, she fixed me with a smile that sent my thoughts careering in all sorts of ungentlemanly directions.

"See you in the morning, Mr. Pearce."

She left me standing in the hall, my brow slick with sweat and my eyes lingering over her receding form. When she'd rounded the corner and disappeared from view, I let myself into my chamber.

But it was a long time before sleep took me.

Six

The morning began poorly. I peered out my window at a countryside enshrouded in an impenetrable fog. I couldn't imagine venturing out into it without tethering myself to a familiar object.

We received breakfast in our quarters, a fact for which I would have been thankful had the eggs been warmer and the orange juice less tepid. The serving maid lowered her eyes in apology after she'd placed the tray on my bedside table. "I was ready to deliver your victuals earlier, but Miss Violet insisted you preferred your food sit for a spell before digging in."

I arched an eyebrow. "Have you known anyone who prefers cold eggs over warm?"

She averted her eyes. "Never, Mr. Pearce. I'm ever so sorry."

"And you need not be," I reassured her. "You were only doing what your mistress bade."

Seeing I was in earnest, she flashed me a grateful smile before departing. But that didn't render the eggs any less slimy.

The next disturbing portent occurred when I rounded the corner into the Great Hall and found Sarah speaking to an older man.

The same man I'd observed torturing the cat.

Jonathan Janz

As I approached them, Sarah uttered the damning words. "Why hello, Arthur. I'd like you to meet Tom Erskine."

His face no longer blood-spattered and leering, Erskine nodded and extended a hand.

I ignored it. "Fed your hounds yet?"

If Erskine intuited my meaning, he gave no sign. "Not till midmorning, sir. I like 'em to work up an appetite."

"Does that give you time to scare up defenseless animals?"

Erskine's eyes narrowed.

Sarah watched me with a look of dismay. "Why, Arthur... you speak as though Tom has wronged you."

My voice grew raw around the edges. "A man who revels in the anguish of an innocent creature does harm to the universe. Mr. Erskine is not who you think he is."

Erskine stepped toward me. "Listen here, youngster. You'll not traipse into this house and spit accusations—"

"Good morning, Arthur!" a voice called.

It was Hubert Coyle. He looked dapper in his light gray suit and matching bowler hat.

Taking no note of the enmity between me and his head groom, Hubert raised a glossy black cane and said, "I don't need this walking stick, but Juniper insists it complements the outfit." He brandished it dourly. "A silly affectation."

"I agree with Mother," Sarah said. She cast an uneasy glance at me before turning her attentions to her father's overcoat, which she smoothed with affection. "You look positively genteel, Father."

Hubert smiled. "I suppose looks can deceive, can they not?"

"Yes," I said, facing Erskine. "They certainly can."

Erskine looked as though he yearned to feed me to his hounds.

"And Juniper," Hubert said, arms spread. Mrs. Coyle joined us in the Great Hall, her dark locks pinned beneath a pale green hat. Her dress was lime green, and she carried a spindly white parasol.

The Dismembered

Violet was next to join us, followed by Jimmy, whose haggard complexion and half-lidded eyes bespoke of too much drink and too little food. We moved into the marble foyer, Hubert's cane tip clacking like a poorly-wound clock.

"Of all mornings, Jimmy," Violet scolded, "couldn't you have made yourself presentable this once?"

"I hardly see the relevance of my appearance, Sister Dear. I'm not the one Mr. Dunning wishes to defile next Saturday night."

"If he's not done so already," Sarah added in an undertone.

Mrs. Coyle gasped. "Sarah!"

Violet drew herself up. "It's fine, Mother. She's merely bitter she has no Count of her own and must resort to picking up stragglers on trains."

Hubert winced. "Please, Violet. There's no need to insult Mr. Pearce. He's a good soul, and a learned one. I respect writers."

Violet regarded me with open contempt. "What makes you think he has any talent, Father? For all we know, he's no more an author than Jimmy here."

"He is," someone said to our left. We looked up and beheld Lizzie descending the curved staircase. She had discarded the black evening gown in favor of a simpler black dress. However, the manner in which it hugged her lithe body recalled the sight of her bare thigh from the night before. I looked away quickly so as not to be branded a wolf.

"Poor Lizzie," Violet said, the corners of her mouth downturned, "I had hoped you'd remain at Altarbrook this morning."

As Lizzie continued down the stairs, she tugged on a pair of black gloves. "And miss an opportunity to tour the enigmatic Castle Magnus?"

Sarah watched her older sister with a look no less disdainful than the one Violet wore. "We'd hoped to marry you off to some unsuspecting suitor a decade ago. Now we're stuck with you."

"Oh, lay off her," Jimmy moaned. "Your sniping makes my head throb."

"That's the absinthe," Violet said. "Our sniping only reminds you of what failures the eldest Coyle children are."

Hubert waved his cane in exasperation. "Could we *please* desist in this warfare? You go at one another like a pack of hounds."

Mrs. Coyle fingered her parasol thoughtfully. "What did you mean just now, Lizzie? About Mr. Pearce and his writing?"

Lizzie stepped off the final stair and approached us. She was tall, only an inch or two shorter than me, and the manner in which she'd tied her hair back accentuated her prominent cheekbones and striking blue eyes. I wondered how she'd reached her late twenties unwed.

"Last night," she said, "I thought Mr. Pearce's name familiar. Later on, I finally recollected where I'd seen it." She looked at me. "You were in *Pearson's*."

"Yes," I answered.

"On three occasions."

"Four, actually."

A barely perceptible nod. "Father allowed our subscription to lapse one summer. I expect that explains the missing tale."

Mrs. Coyle was looking at me in astonishment. She said to Lizzie, "You've read Mr. Pearce's work?"

Violet was scowling. "What on earth is *Pearson's*?"

"One of the most influential literary magazines in the world," Lizzie explained. "There's an English version and an American one. Have you been published in both, Mr. Pearce?"

"I have."

"More allegory?"

I hesitated. "I'm afraid you've confused me with another writer."

"No confusion," she said. "'An Empty Hat in the Park'?"

Hearing one of my titles on her lips disconcerted me. "That was inspired by my experience at a small country newspaper."

The Dismembered

"It was the least of the three," Lizzie said, her gaze unwavering. "The best was 'Guillotine.' That tale was what compelled me to read your novel."

I couldn't conceal my shock. "You've read it?"

"I hadn't," she said. "Until last night."

Hubert's grin was so admiring I worried he might request an autograph. "Of all the miraculous coincidences! How was it, Dear?"

"Oh, who *cares* how it was," Violet snapped. "We're late."

I started at Violet's tone. Truth be told, I had forgotten the others were present.

Violet stalked toward the door, which a butler opened. She disappeared into the hungry gray fog. Jimmy shambled after her, a hand visoring his eyes against the daylight. Lizzie continued to study me with an interest to which I was unaccustomed. As self-pitying as it might sound, my ex-wife had acclimated me to aloofness.

Sarah's arm twined around my own, and she gave Lizzie a pointed look. "Let us journey to Castle Magnus," Sarah said. "We have much to accomplish today, do we not?"

Mrs. Coyle drew back. "What an odd way to put it."

"Come, Arthur," Sarah said, prying me away.

I didn't have to glance backward to know Lizzie was still watching me.

Seven

One of my favorite passages in literature is the opening of Poe's yarn of melancholy suspense, "The Fall of the House of Usher." And perhaps because of this affinity, I expected to have the same reaction to Castle Magnus as Poe's narrator had to the ill-fated dwelling. Yet it wasn't desolation or sorrow that gripped me as our coach drew closer.

It was dread.

In every way Dunning's castle was Altarbrook's antithesis. Where Altarbrook boasted respectability and symmetry, Castle Magnus exuded chaos and angularity. Perched atop a sheer cliff, the structure resembled a clutch of stalagmites jutting from a craggy mountain plateau. The sooty stone façade and multitudinous spires engendered a sensation of vertigo, one that made me yearn to flee.

"Lovely, isn't it?" Violet asked.

Yes, I thought. *For a ghoul.*

Violet stared through the window, the swirling fog at times revealing the castle, at others rendering it as insubstantial as a wraith. "Richard's ancestors oversaw the completion of the structure."

"Must have been a dangerous task," I remarked.

Jonathan Janz

"I don't doubt a workman or two lost his life, but the result is majestic."

"I wonder how the workmen's families felt about the castle's majesty," Lizzie mused.

"Oh, do cease carping, Lizzie," Violet said. "The least you can do is pretend to be happy for me."

We bounced over a pothole, and Jimmy groaned.

Lizzie's glance was not unkind. "Did you take something for it, Jimmy?"

"Nothing that agreed with me," he moaned.

Violet stared daggers at her brother. "Richard believes intemperance is the mark of an inferior intellect."

Lizzie brushed a stray lock from Jimmy's forehead. "And generalizing is a sign of genius?"

Sarah glared at Lizzie. "Some might argue your defense of Jimmy encourages his self-destruction."

Jimmy produced a small bottle of absinthe, tilted it to empty. He cast aside the bottle and said, "Lizzie's the only one who doesn't expend her energy conniving."

Violet whirled in her seat. "Go to hell, Jimmy."

"Ah, we're here," Hubert said.

I exhaled. Had we remained within the coach's confines any longer, the siblings might have gouged one another's eyes out.

As we disembarked, I heard the clopping of hooves, cast about for the source of the noise, for our own carriage horses were reposing silently in the shadow of Castle Magnus.

"Ah, Tom!" Hubert said.

Lizzie stiffened. "Why is he here?"

Hubert smiled in bemusement. "Why, to tend to our needs, of course. Violet tells us we'll be exploring the grounds. Should one of you grow fatigued and require a ride back, Tom can provide assistance."

I took Sarah by the arm and steered her away. "There's something you need to know about Mr. Erskine."

The Dismembered

"What do you have against Tom?"

"Only his excessive cruelty," I responded. "Last night I witnessed a scene so abhorrent that I shudder to—"

"You've arrived!" a voice boomed from the castle doorstep.

We all turned and beheld a tall, strapping man in an ebony suit. His black, wavy hair glistened with oil, his strong jaw shaped as by an artisan's chisel. I half-expected him to sport a top hat or a flowing cape, but his head was bare and his black suit coat unadorned. He glided across the driveway with the grace of an athlete, and as he approached us it seemed that the very air grew charged as though a thunderstorm attended his steps. He bowed to Mrs. Coyle, who placed a hand on her chest in a near-swoon.

A sly strategy, I decided, *to entrance the mother-in-law first.*

He shook hands warmly with Hubert, continued to Jimmy, who muttered something unintelligible, before reaching Violet, over whom a noticeable change had come. Gone was the thorny defiance she'd exhibited in the coach; in its place radiated a devotion that was unsettling.

"My dear Violet," Richard Dunning said, enveloping her hands in his. "Your beauty cleaves this obscuring veil and enthralls me with its clarion glow."

Lizzie crossed her arms. "The glow you're talking about is adolescence."

Violet darkened with rage, but Dunning merely smiled. "You must be Elizabeth. Violet has shared much about you."

"Rather surprising," Jimmy said. "The two never talk without their hands about each other's throats."

Dunning nodded at Violet's siblings. "I know you're not in favor of my marriage suit, and I sincerely appreciate your protectiveness of your baby sister."

"What do you know of sincerity?" Sarah asked.

Hubert cleared his throat. "Violet tells me your lake provides excellent fishing."

Jonathan Janz

Dunning lowered his eyes. "I fear I must disappoint you, Mr. Coyle. The fog precludes us from wandering the grounds."

"Thank God," Jimmy muttered.

His mother tilted her head reprovingly. "You know, Jimmy, you might not be so light-sensitive if you exercised moderation."

Violet barked out a laugh, but Dunning placed a solicitous hand on Jimmy's shoulder. Until that moment I hadn't noticed how imposing a figure the Count cut; he positively dwarfed Jimmy.

Dunning said, "Would you care to take a rest in one of our drawing rooms, Jimmy? I quite understand the effects of absinthe."

Sarah stepped forward, clasped her brother by the arm, and led him away from the Count. "I think it ill-advised to separate from the party, Jimmy. I shall accompany you if you need support."

Jimmy massaged his forehead. "Can you lessen this infernal pounding in my skull?"

Looking abashed, Mr. and Mrs. Coyle followed Sarah and Jimmy inside.

Violet turned her icy stare on Lizzie. "Well, Dearest Sister, it looks like we're to enter Castle Magnus together. I would be indebted if you'd feign civility."

Lizzie watched after her parents, who'd already begun to utter hushed praise of the castle's entryway. "Civility is unnatural," she murmured. She glanced at Violet's midsection. "As is abdominal strangulation. Have you considered the long-term hazards of such violent corseting?"

Violet smiled nastily. "Better to be slightly bundled than to resemble a sack of flour. Then again, were I approaching middle age and had no viable suitors, I might cease maintaining my appearance as well."

Unruffled, Lizzie arched an eyebrow. "Have you slept with him yet?"

The Dismembered

Dunning was several feet off conversing with Tom Erskine, and appeared unaware of Lizzie's scandalous inquiry. I, on the other hand, found myself trapped between the sisters.

Violet's lips thinned. "What Richard and I do is none of your concern."

"A virgin then," Lizzie said. "Trust me, sex is overrated. You're better off using those delicate fingers to sate your desires."

I went several shades redder.

Violet's teeth showed. "Why you foul-mouthed *Jezebel*." A glance in my direction. "How can you utter such filth in the presence of a guest?"

Lizzie answered, "Like many divorced people, Mr. Pearce understands the pitfalls of carnal desires."

I stood thunderstruck, with nary a clue how to respond. How could Lizzie know of Angela and our doomed marriage? My mind raced for possible explanations. There had been brief biographies in the stories published in *Pearson's Literary Magazine*, but none of them had mentioned my marital status.

Violet shot a look at her fiancé, who was now approaching, then favored Lizzie with a cagey gleam. "Have it your way, Lizzie," she said, starting up the porch steps. "At least do me the courtesy of entering the home in which, according to you, I will experience so much consternation."

Lizzie followed Violet inside.

Count Dunning drew even with me on the bottom porch step. "Mr. Erskine tells me you're an author."

I gazed up at the Count, who was two or three inches taller than me and a good deal broader. "I'm between novels," I managed.

"Perhaps you'll find inspiration at Castle Magnus."

I peered up at its rising spires. "I do admit it's arresting."

He followed my gaze. "Yes…arresting. Its contours suggest disorder, do they not?"

Jonathan Janz

I looked at him, surprised to have my thoughts so accurately expressed. "Who was the architect?"

He appeared not to hear me. "Shall we join the others, Mr. Pearce?"

As we entered the castle, the baying of dogs reached my ears. "Are there wild animals on your lands, Mr. Dunning?"

He grinned. "Aren't all animals wild at heart, Mr. Pearce?"

We stepped inside, and the massive doors closed behind us.

Part TWO

Castle Magnus

Eight

Count Dunning proved a perfectly suitable host, leading us first on a tour of the main floor, then belowground into a labyrinth of tunnels. Hubert and his wife followed Violet and the Count down the stone steps, which were clammy with grit. Next came Sarah and I, with Lizzie and Jimmy bringing up the rear.

Violet clung to her fiancé's arm. "Why ever would you lead us down here, Richard?"

Dunning nodded my way. "As an aficionado of the macabre, I thought Mr. Pearce would appreciate the catacombs."

I glanced at Sarah. "My reputation seems to have preceded me."

As we advanced down a gloomy corridor, the flickering wall torches revealed a series of barred cells.

"I trust this isn't where you house your guests," Hubert remarked.

Dunning favored Violet with a slight grin. "Only when they're naughty."

Violet giggled and nuzzled the Count's shoulder, the quintessence of the infatuated teenage girl. I experienced a twinge of disgust. With his worldly magnetism, I understood how Dunning

Jonathan Janz

could inveigle an impressionable young woman. Yet as inappropriate as I found the match, Violet's parents appeared to approve. They beamed at one another as though Dunning were heaven sent. Considering their financial difficulties, I supposed he was.

Sarah, however, watched the lovers with open contempt. "It's detestable," she muttered. "How can Father allow Violet to be defiled by that fiend?"

"Sarah," I said, taking care to keep my voice low, "how can you be certain that Mr. Erskine's tale about Dunning is credible?"

"Who would concoct such a ghastly story?" she asked, then favored me with an impish smile. "Other than authors who revel in disturbing subjects?"

She leaned into me a bit, and at the brush of her shoulder, I experienced a thrill of pleasure. For the past hour or so I'd forgotten my original aim in journeying to Altarbrook.

Refocused by Sarah's affection, I said to Dunning, "What need have you of barred cells? I would have thought these would've been converted long ago."

"Converted to what?" Dunning challenged. "The electricity does not run down here. The air is too damp for living quarters."

"It's like a tomb," Mrs. Coyle said, peering about with a look of distaste.

"I'd live down here," Jimmy said from behind us. "It's serene, private. No accursed sun assaulting you."

Dunning grinned over his shoulder. "Perhaps we'll make you a permanent resident."

"Is your liquor cabinet well-stocked?" Sarah asked.

Jimmy winked at her. "Thanks for looking out for me, Sis."

As we continued down a dank corridor, Hubert asked, "Were there really prisoners kept in the cells?"

"Some," Dunning answered. "There were once skirmishes between the families of the region."

"So your forefathers locked them up?" Lizzie asked.

The Dismembered

"When someone is trying to kill you," Dunning said, "it's inadvisable to invite them in for tea."

"Unless you're Richard Dunning," Sarah muttered.

"My hearing is quite acute," Dunning said without turning. "Miss Sarah, I'm wholly aware of your rancor."

"Then perhaps you would be so kind to allow us to breath wholesome air again," Sarah said. "I don't relish the idea of being trapped down here with you, however skillfully you may have ensnared my sister."

Violet whirled. "You petty *wench*."

Hubert looked pained. "Please, girls, let's not—"

"It's perfectly all right," Dunning said. "I understand Sarah's apprehension and wish to address it."

Violet looked imploringly at her fiancé. "But Richard, why credit such wild tales? Your character is unimpeachable."

"Quite right," Mrs. Coyle agreed.

"Your work in the village has saved lives," Violet continued. "The hospital, the school, the library...none of these would survive without your patronage."

Dunning smiled humbly. "You do me credit, my flower. Yet I think it time to coax these rumors to the surface, where they can wither in the unblinking light of truth."

"Speaking of flowery," Lizzie muttered.

The Count said, "I brought you all down here to illustrate a point."

"That your ancestors were as sadistic as you?" Sarah asked.

"*Sarah*," Hubert said.

Dunning went on, unperturbed. "That love cannot thrive in darkness." He indicated the cells with a sweeping gesture. "You are all slaves to negative emotions." He glanced at Hubert and Juniper. "Worry." A look at Sarah. "Suspicion." At me. "Self-doubt." He nodded at Jimmy. "A lack of industry."

Violet frowned. "You left Lizzie out. Surely you don't find her above base emotions?"

Jonathan Janz

"I find Lizzie uncommonly perceptive," Dunning said.

Violet looked stricken, but Lizzie didn't answer.

"Come, all," Dunning said briskly. "It's time for you to emerge from your shadows. The Eastern Spire is just the place for such a cleansing."

Nine

The climb up the winding spiral staircase proved arduous for Jimmy, who required several stops along the way. By the third story, the others grew exasperated with his lagging, so I volunteered to accompany him the rest of the way up the Eastern Spire, which according to Dunning was no fewer than nine stories high.

We'd made it halfway up the next flight of stairs when Jimmy slumped against the wooden banister with a groan. "I think we might behold a resurfacing of last night's roast."

"Not to be judgmental, Jimmy, but why do you inflict such damage on yourself?"

Head on forearm, Jimmy answered, "You assume my consumption is volitional, Mr. Pearce. I don't expect you to understand."

"You might be surprised to learn that I do understand. When I was Violet's age, I fell prey to the demon opium."

For the first time, Jimmy looked me in the eyes. "Go on."

I glanced up the staircase to make sure no one could overhear, found the area empty, but nevertheless went on sotto voce. "Poe suffered from addictions to various substances, opium not the least of which. Though I'm loath to confess it, I adopted similar behaviors, in my naiveté believing such emulation would result in similar genius."

Jimmy grew thoughtful. "Lizzie tells me you're an extraordinary writer."

I was rendered speechless.

A corner of his mouth twitched. "You *do* suffer from self-doubt."

At mention of the Count's diagnosis, some of my pleasure at hearing Lizzie's compliment dissipated. "Dunning seems to relish playing the psychologist."

"Mad scientist is more like it. You'll notice he hasn't mentioned the Western Tower."

"The tallest one?"

"Rumor has it that's where he performs his experiments."

I drew closer. "So you agree the Count is unsuitable?"

Jimmy made a scoffing sound. "Is a wolf suitable as a house pet?"

"But what exactly is the nature of these experiments to which you and Sarah keep alluding?"

Jimmy pushed himself erect. "We should join the others."

"Please don't mention my youthful transgressions to Sarah." I frowned. "Or Lizzie."

Jimmy paused in mid-step. "I'd advise caution, Mr. Pearce. You're wading into deep waters."

I shouldered past him. "I hardly think threatening me is necessary."

He laughed. "Is that what you think I'm doing?"

"Aren't you?"

"There are many varieties of addiction, Mr. Pearce, not all of them opium and absinthe."

Disquieted, I gave no answer, and after several more delays, we reached the zenith of the Eastern Spire.

A stranger reliquary I had never encountered.

The Coyles had scattered throughout the large space, which was cylindrical, at least sixty feet wide, and equipped

The Dismembered

with an open iron staircase that serpentined along the walls before reaching its terminus at the tapered pinnacle of the spire. In addition to a voluminous collection of leatherbound books that surpassed even the Altarbrook library, the Eastern Spire boasted statues, paintings, and various birds of prey, stuffed and suspended from the ceiling at varying heights. The general impression conveyed by the artwork and avian taxidermy was spine tingling.

Dunning approached. "Are your sensibilities offended by my décor, Mr. Pearce? I would've thought you, of all people, would appreciate a darker aesthetic."

"It's morbid."

He raised his eyebrows. "And what do you make of the lovely Miss Sarah?"

I stiffened. "That's none of your concern."

Dunning smirked. "I thought you only met yesterday."

"I'm a keen judge of character, Mr. Dunning, which is why I'd prefer not to share personal observations with you."

"What of Elizabeth?" he asked.

I scowled at him. "What of her?"

"She's fuller-bodied than her sisters, but such widening is to be expected beyond a certain age."

I opened my mouth to respond, but Jimmy, about whom I'd completely forgotten, said, "Mind your tongue about Lizzie. Her body is none of your business, Dunning."

I glanced at Jimmy with new appreciation, but Dunning merely favored him with a humoring grin. "My young man, you misunderstand me. One of my specialties is human physiognomy. Your Elizabeth is a fascinating specimen."

"Specimen?" Jimmy demanded.

The Count nodded toward where she stood, her back to us, her bare shoulder blades shifting as she paged through a book. "Not a traditional beauty, but striking in her own way. The lines of her neck…the smoothness of her skin…long-limbed…"

He nodded. "Yes, her arms and legs, particularly, strike me as interesting."

I clenched my jaws. "Shouldn't your eyes be directed toward your fiancé?"

Dunning nodded faintly, but his gaze upon Lizzie did not waver. "Violet possesses several interesting features. Her hands, her ears." He glanced at Jimmy. "You both have the slender Coyle throat."

Frowning, Jimmy massaged his neck.

A servant appeared at that moment, a sallow-faced man of middling years, and bade Dunning meet with some visitor downstairs. On the way out, the Count encouraged us to examine the furnishings, and we soon lapsed into a companionable silence. I wandered toward a long case of books, most of them treatises on the occult and ancient alchemy, and it wasn't until I stood next to Lizzie that I realized I'd been gravitating in her direction.

"You read my novel," I said under my breath.

"So did Dunning," Lizzie answered.

I blinked at her. She gestured toward a russet-colored tome housed on an aged bronze stand.

"Coincidence," I murmured.

"Was it coincidence when Douglas met Edith?"

I turned toward her, astonished to hear her reference the central relationship in my only published novel. Bemused, I said, "But that didn't end well, did it."

"The ending made me happy."

I squinted at her. "She murdered him."

"Precisely. I was afraid you'd force them to stay together."

I selected a book from the shelf and pretended to study it. "Is your opinion of marriage so cynical?"

Her gaze lifted to the hawks and owls dangling overhead. "We're surrounded by predators, Mr. Pearce. I'm sure you know that, given your experience."

This was too much. "How did you know I was married?"

The Dismembered

She gave me a disbelieving look. "Why, Douglas and Edith, of course. One could only write a tragic relationship with such authority if he'd already tasted the bitterness of betrayal."

My voice grew hoarse. "My wife and I were together when I wrote that."

"But you suspected," she said, "even if you hadn't yet accepted the truth."

I closed the book with an audible clap. "If you're such an expert on marital relations, how is it you've no experience yourself?"

"I've been in relationships."

"But—"

"Several relationships."

She was gazing at me now. I found myself sweating.

She nodded at my book. "The Count wants you to know he read this."

"I suppose you have a theory as to why?"

"Power. Control. It always comes down to those urges. Even sexual desire is traceable to control."

Having never heard someone speak so boldly, I couldn't conceal my discomfiture. Yet it wasn't disapproval I was feeling, for there was something deliciously untamed in Lizzie Coyle, something liberating. So many times I had privately bewailed humankind's tendency to take refuge in the unspoken. How many disasters might be averted if people would simply say what they mean?

"Do you disapprove of Violet's engagement?" I asked.

A pause. "Violet is of age."

I selected a slender black volume and pretended to thumb through the pages. "Apparently, evasiveness is a universal tendency as well."

"You want me to impugn the Count's character?"

I tapped a picture in the volume I held. "I had no idea the mummification process was so complex."

"I do not believe Dunning's nature is consistent with his public face," she said, her words clipped. "There are many stories, Mr. Pearce, some so outlandish they make your 'Sexton's Song' seem plausible."

Though it wasn't a compliment—was, if anything, a condemnation of my second story in *Pearson's*—I smiled at the allusion. Hearing my work referenced was a novelty to which I was unaccustomed.

"Do I approve of the Count?" she went on. "I believe him a manipulative dissimulator who is preying on my baby sister, no matter what an insufferable brat she happens to be. Do I trust Richard Dunning? I no more trust him than I trust you, Mr. Pearce, a man who journeyed to Altarbrook under the auspices of providing aid to Sarah, when in truth you're enslaved by your sexual organs."

"I hardly think my sexual organs are a subject for polite conversation."

"Fuck politeness."

I gawked at her. Not even Angela, in her most venomous moods, had used that epithet with me. Only during my rambles on the Boston wharfs had I heard the word uttered with such temerity.

She scowled. "Oh, don't look so scandalized, Mr. Pearce. As a writer, surely you're willing to squirm in the muck and..." she trailed off, her eyes shifting to something behind me. "I didn't see you..."

It was the Count. He'd reentered the Eastern Spire as silently as an autumn breeze. I immediately replayed my confrontation with Lizzie, racking my brain to judge what he'd heard.

Before I could properly assess the damage, Dunning announced, "All is in order. It's time for us to indulge our appetites."

Ten

As we sat to dinner at the lengthy dark-grained table, I again found myself contrasting Castle Magnus and Altarbrook. The dining room in the Coyle residence was a warm, inviting place resplendent with Impressionist art and green flock wallpaper. The dining hall at Castle Magnus resembled an inquisitorial torture chamber. The walls were bloodred, the floor raven-colored stone. Maces and scimitars depended from the ceiling, giving one the impression that punishment for some sin was imminent. The weaponry continued along the walls, where armored figures brandished jousts and broadswords. From the accouterment of ancient warfare to the murkiness of the table itself, the dining hall did little to stimulate the appetite. That is, I decided, unless one were a cannibal, and the reminders of human barbarism made one's stomach growl.

Count Dunning evidently noticed my scrutiny of the table, for he remarked, "Yew wood, Mr. Pearce. Coarse and pitted, it is nevertheless a reminder of my heritage."

Lizzie asked, "Isn't the yew tree purported to possess talismanic qualities?"

"It is," Dunning answered, pleased. "Violet told me you're a reader."

"Snob is more like it," Violet muttered.

"Now Darling," Dunning said to Violet, who was seated to his immediate right, "you need to appreciate your elder sister. You won't be together much longer."

At the word 'elder,' Lizzie's eyes narrowed, but it was the Count's final sentence that disquieted me. Granted, Violet would soon be leaving her parents' home, but something about the Count's tone...

"Might we be treated to a beverage with more character than tea?" Jimmy drawled.

Dunning favored him with a look of amusement. "You'd prefer port, maybe?"

"I would," Jimmy agreed.

The Count tipped a nod toward a servant, who disappeared. "We'll bring in Broxton. He is my vintner and my authority on all forms of drink. He'll provide a selection of ales and lagers."

Jimmy grinned. "I like this Broxton fellow already."

Dunning turned. "How is your salad, Mrs. Coyle?"

"Sublime," she answered.

Hubert said, "You must have your cook share the recipe for this dressing."

Lizzie, who sat to my right, muttered something I couldn't make out. Before I could ask her to repeat it, Dunning said, "Rudeness."

We all stopped chewing.

Hubert smiled. "I beg your pardon, Mr. Dunning?"

"You heard me," Dunning said, all hospitality having fled from his face. His gaze upon Lizzie was stony. "Repeat your insult so your family can hear it."

Mrs. Coyle put a hand to her chest. "Why, Lizzie. Whatever did you say?"

Lizzie set down her fork and met Dunning's hostile expression. "'He won't tell you,' is what I said. Meaning, you won't share the recipe for your salad dressing."

The Dismembered

Hubert sat back. "Was that all? I admit, Count Dunning, it was an odd remark, but I hardly think it reason for indignation."

The heat of Dunning's gaze did not diminish. "Ask your daughter what she's implying."

Lizzie said, "I'm implying you guard your secrets."

"Is discretion a crime, Miss Elizabeth?"

"Yes," she answered, "given that our families are to be united in marriage within a week."

Hubert dabbed his mouth with a napkin, which was the same bloodred hue as the walls. "I agree with Lizzie, Count Dunning. The public persona you've fostered does seem at odds with your habitation."

Dunning's look hardened. "You attack me in my own home."

Hubert flushed. "I only mean to say it gives one pause. After all, I am promising my youngest daughter to you. I think I deserve some insight into your character."

Dunning's upper lip curled. "The only thing you deserve is a hard slap, Mr. Coyle."

Hubert gaped at Dunning.

"Miserable little cur," Dunning growled. "Selling off his daughter to save his estate."

"Hah!" Jimmy laughed. "Now we get to it."

Dunning said, "Enter, Broxton."

I felt my blood freeze. The man bearing the tray was enormous, bearded, and totally unsmiling.

"Wonderful!" Jimmy said. "Come, Broxton. I shall be happy to sample them all."

But I scarcely registered Jimmy's invitation.

For Broxton was the brute from the train.

Eleven

I peered at Sarah, but she wasn't looking at me, and seated as she was beside Dunning, she was too far away for me to address without the others hearing. I decided I didn't care if the others heard me. Finding myself face-to-face with the man who accosted Sarah on the train was too disconcerting to ignore.

"Count Dunning," I began, "it might interest you to know that your 'vintner,' as you refer to this villain, attempted to rob your soon-to-be sister-in-law."

Dunning smiled. "Impossible."

"Unless he has a twin brother," I persisted, "he is absolutely the same scoundrel."

"Broxton?" Dunning said.

"Sir?" Broxton answered. He loomed over Jimmy, the platter of glasses hovering mere inches from Jimmy's face, as if to tantalize the inveterate drinker with promises of oblivion.

As Jimmy selected a glass of some marshy-looking liquid and guzzled half of it at a draught, Dunning nodded at Lizzie and me. "The two of you are intent on defaming me."

I glanced at Sarah, waiting for her to corroborate my claim, but inexplicably, she was gazing at her plate as though adrift in other thoughts.

Dunning spread his hands. "Why don't you share your suspicions with the group?"

Lizzie frowned. "Suspicions?"

Dunning folded a leg over his knee. "Oh come now, Miss Elizabeth, you know the rumors to which I'm referring. There are several besotted villagers who whisper about me like I'm Satan himself."

Jimmy downed the rest of his drink, wiped his mouth theatrically, and flourished his glass. "The devil couldn't create a port this delectable. Another, Broxton!"

Broxton placed another glass before Jimmy. "A radiant color," Jimmy commented. He held it up to the light. "The elixir of Castle Magnus. May your healing potions soothe these weary veins."

Lizzie addressed the Count. "If you're referring to the rumors of your age, I'm afraid I can't verify or dispute them."

Dunning pushed to his feet, his height and impressive musculature surpassing even Broxton's. "I'm not asking you to verify them...merely to verbalize them. Your mother, for instance, has likely not heard the legends. And your father, if he has been privy to them, has convinced himself they're unfounded in order to preserve his impending financial salvation."

Jimmy slugged back another drink and sighed. "Immaculate."

Hubert looked ill. "Could we please not talk about my finances?"

Dunning moved closer to Violet. "Everyone knows Altarbrook teeters on the brink of extinction. But they don't know what role I've played in its demise."

Hubert's look of befuddlement would have been comical had it not been so pitiful.

Violet peered over her shoulder at her fiancé. "Richard, dear, whatever do you mean?"

But Dunning's attention was riveted on Lizzie. "Afraid of uttering the rumors, Miss Elizabeth, lest they prove true?"

The Dismembered

Lizzie cleared her throat. "Some say you're a murderer, Mr. Dunning."

Dunning grinned. "*Just* a murderer, Miss Elizabeth? Surely such whispers contain more phantasmagorical shadings than simple murder."

"They say you dissect people. That you harvest their body parts."

I thought of Tom Erskine's story and felt the hackles on my neck rise.

"You can have my body parts if you fancy them," Jimmy said, alcohol dribbling down his chin. "Though I doubt you'll desire my liver!"

Dunning moved behind Mrs. Coyle, his eyes blazing. "Go on, Miss Elizabeth."

"There was a girl in town," Lizzie continued. "An unfortunate charwoman who'd fallen into prostitution to buy medicine for her ailing daughter."

Dunning nodded. "And what did I do to her?"

I could feel the heat baking off of Lizzie, but her voice remained steady. "You removed her left leg. Or so the villagers say."

Violet sniffed loudly, drawing all our attention.

Mrs. Coyle turned to her youngest daughter. "What is it, Violet? Do you need to lie down?"

Violet murmured something unintelligible. Dunning continued along the table, where the shadows were thickest.

Jimmy chose an amber-colored glass, took a drink, and swished it around his mouth. "Not as full-bodied as the dark, but no less enchanting. I detect a fruity quality. It imparts a sensation of mischief. I must pursue the matter further..." He tilted the glass.

"And these faceless rumormongers," Dunning said, "what do they claim I do with these harvested body parts? Decorate my castle with them? Feed them to my guests?"

Jonathan Janz

"I don't feel well," Hubert said.

"You told me it was necessary," Violet murmured.

Mrs. Coyle rubbed her daughter's hand. "What was necessary, my dear?"

"The construction of a new being," Lizzie answered.

Dunning approached Jimmy. "Ah, the Frankenstein legend!" A wide-eyed glance at me. "We've ventured into your territory, Mr. Pearce. I assume you're familiar with Miss Shelley's masterpiece?"

"Of course," I answered.

"But sadly, it's a work of fiction," Dunning said.

"The quality of this lager is no fiction," Jimmy remarked. "Hit me again Broxton."

Broxton complied.

I could stomach it no longer. I sat forward and addressed the vintner. "You belong in jail, sir. How dare you stand in Sarah's presence after terrorizing her?"

An unsavory smile formed on Broxton's bearded lips.

Lizzie remained focused on the Count. "Shelley deemed her Dr. Frankenstein a Modern Prometheus because he meddled with forces beyond his control. He attempted to play God."

Dunning's eyes gleamed. "And you believe I harbor similar aspirations?"

"I believe you are mad," Lizzie answered.

"Mad?" Dunning uttered a harsh laugh. "Madness implies a rudderless drifting, an absence of purpose."

Violet choked out a sob. Tears shone in her eyes.

Mrs. Coyle ceased her ministrations on Violet's hand. "That's strange," she said in a faraway voice.

Dunning ignored her. "The problem with the Coyles is their lack of appreciation."

"I appreciate the hell out of this glass," Jimmy said, toasting.

Broxton's smile became more pronounced.

The Dismembered

I glowered at the impudent brute. "I shall notify the authorities of your behavior on the train."

Dunning ignored me. "They don't appreciate their home. They don't appreciate their lands."

Mrs. Coyle's voice was tight. "Violet, what's the matter with your—"

"They don't appreciate beauty," Dunning went on. "The simple poetry of the human body."

Broxton was positively leering at me now.

Dunning detached a hanging scimitar from its string and ran a thumb over its edge. "Behold the craftsmanship of this blade. The sturdiness of its handle."

"I'm sorry, Mother," Violet said. "Had I known…"

Dunning pointed the sword at Lizzie. "Yet it doesn't compare to the sensuous lines of an arm." His eyes lowered. "The supple curve of a breast."

"Now see here," I said.

Dunning placed a hand on Jimmy's hair and nudged his head sideways. "The delicate, swanlike neck."

Violet rose. Began tugging at the glove on her right hand. "I trusted your wisdom, Richard."

"Oh Jesus," Lizzie said.

Violet's glove slid slower, one tug at a time.

Sarah finally looked up. "Violet, don't!"

Violet pulled the glove off, revealing a burnished wooden prosthetic. Mrs. Coyle gasped.

I turned toward Dunning.

"Don't—" I began, but Dunning had already lashed out with the sword. He sliced through Jimmy's neck below the jaw. Blood erupted from Jimmy's throat like a geyser, the scarlet fountain drenching Broxton, Dunning, and Hubert Coyle, who had tumbled out of his chair, away from his decapitated son. Mrs. Coyle screamed. Violet collapsed on the table, the *thunk* of her wooden hand as loud as an axe blow.

Jonathan Janz

"Just one more," Dunning said and cast the severed head aside. He braced himself, whipped the scimitar in a backhand stroke, and sliced Jimmy's neck off at the shoulders.

"Good one, sir!" Broxton shouted.

"I'm sorry!" Violet wailed. "I didn't know!"

Dunning raised the neatly-severed neck and inspected it. "Even lovelier than Violet's. I'm so happy Jimmy dragged his carcass out of bed this morning."

Hubert was gaping at his son's body, which had slumped onto the table and was pumping blood all over Jimmy's uneaten salad. "My son…" Hubert whispered. "You…killed my boy."

Lizzie sobbed. I wanted to comfort her but was too aghast to move.

"Yes," Dunning said, turning the dripping neck this way and that. "This will do nicely."

"Jimmy," Violet said, her voice breaking.

It was then that I noticed Sarah's expression. While the rest of us were looking on in horrorstruck silence, Sarah had been rising to her feet and striding toward Dunning. I expected her to retaliate, to avenge her dead brother.

Instead, she snaked her arms around Count Dunning, opened her mouth, and tongued the blood from his lips.

Twelve

izzie was the first to move. "You monster!" she
shrieked and was halfway around the table when the
door burst open and a swarm of servants piled into the room.
The gaunt butler intercepted Lizzie before she could stab
Dunning with the steak knife she grasped. Up until then I'd
been too horrified to react, but when Lizzie's knife dropped
to the floor, I retrieved my own steak knife, and slid it inside
my hip pocket.

Dunning's servants fell on me and wrenched me away from
the table. Three stout women in maid's frocks encircled Violet
and Mrs. Coyle. One of the maids, speaking in an Irish brogue,
asked, "What would ya like done with this pair, sir?"

"Why have you deceived me?" Violet beseeched Sarah.

Her mouth smeared with blood—her brother's blood, I
amended with dull horror—Sarah grinned at her baby sister
and said, "In what sane universe would Richard choose you over
me? You're a shrill walkingstick. A petulant child."

Dunning regarded Violet with a pitying glance. "I'm afraid
what she says is true, Violet. You were a means to an end.
Nothing more."

Hubert spoke up, though Broxton's forearm around his neck
garbled his speech. "Please spare my Violet. She's blameless."

Jonathan Janz

Broxton roared laughter.

"There will be no sparing," Dunning said. "The only question will be who perishes last. Take them."

After an endless, nightmarish descent into the bowels of the castle, we found ourselves locked in the cells we'd toured. In the cell adjacent to Mrs. Coyle's lay Violet, who had seemingly lost the will to live. Violet's neighbor was Lizzie, followed by my cell, then Hubert's. A survey of my fellow inmates' faces revealed a wretched band: Mrs. Coyle's hat hung askew, her dark hair stringing over her brow like the tassels of a cheap lampshade. Violet's corseted body tremored with sobs. Hubert looked as though he'd been beaten and robbed in some Lower London alleyway; he kept wincing and grasping his left side. Fractured ribs, I suspected. Lizzie's hair had burst completely free of its pins, her black dress torn in numerous places. Gone was the Sphinxlike smile that had so jangled my nerves upon our first meeting; in its place lurked a raging goddess whose fighting spirit has been roused. Lizzie exuded more vitality than the rest of us combined.

She shook her head. "That treacherous *harpy*. I knew she and Jimmy weren't close, but to engineer his death—"

"We don't know Sarah engineered it," Hubert said.

"It comes to the same thing," Lizzie hissed. "I don't doubt she was obeying Dunning's orders, but her complicity disgusts me."

Her voice inflectionless, Violet said, "Sarah has always been spellbound by the Count."

"How do you mean?" Hubert asked.

"Many were the evenings when Sarah and I would go for rambles to gaze upon Castle Magnus."

Hubert's tone was gentle. "Dear Violet, everyone in the county is fascinated by Castle Magnus. It was hardly abnormal for two children to express curiosity."

"It was more than curiosity," Violet answered. "I was smitten with the Count. His thick, wavy locks…his piercing eyes…I think he was the first man I found attractive."

The Dismembered

A measure of Lizzie's sarcasm resurfaced. "Sarah shared that feeling, apparently."

"You jest, Lizzie, but you don't know Sarah like I do. She's developed this...well, this *obsession* with him." Violet sighed. "I suppose it had to do with winning. I've always been too competitive, particularly where Sarah is concerned..."

She lapsed into morose silence, and I found myself recalling Sarah's tale about the Count bestowing the tiger lily upon her during her childhood. What for many might have been a harmless lark became, in Sarah, an unwholesome mania.

"She's been seeing him every night," Lizzie said, as though to herself.

Mrs. Coyle finally emerged from her grief-stricken fugue. "That's impossible."

"What made you suspect?" Hubert asked.

Lizzie flashed a bitter smile. "A woman can tell, Father. When you taste of profligacy for the first time, it changes you...grinds you down. A light leaves your eyes. In its place grows a shadow."

I studied her. "What happened to you?"

A harsh laugh. "Since we're all going to die, I might as well reveal my scandalous history."

"That's not necessary, Lizzie," her father said.

Violet sat up on her elbows and studied her oldest sister through the bars. "I thought you were a virgin."

Lizzie made a scoffing sound, swept long blond tresses off her ear. "Please, Violet. You really don't know much of the world, do you?"

"No," Violet said, frowning. "I don't suppose I do."

"Five years ago, I grew tired of my cloistered existence at Altarbrook," Lizzie began.

Mrs. Coyle said, "Honey, don't—"

"I found myself in London, twenty-three, alone, with a headful of novels and not a single rational thought. I went home with the first man I met, and I slept with him."

She looked at me in challenge, but if she expected me to be affronted, she found no such satisfaction.

"Please, Lizzie," Hubert said, "we've all made mistakes."

"I had relations with a series of men," Lizzie pushed on. "None of it meant anything to anyone, least of all me. I thought I was being clever. Flouting the hypocritical conventions of our society."

Lizzie paused, and we all remained silent, her parents evidently resigned to her unburdening.

"After six months in London, I was ready to return home. I regretted my actions, not because I wished to conform to the antiquated notions of English womanhood. I…" She grimaced. "…I had dishonored myself with my indiscriminate choice of partners. On the eve of my departure there came a knock on my door. It was Dennis Bridger, a man whose apartment I had visited one night after imbibing too much champagne. He had…" She swallowed, her eyes shimmering with tears. "…testimonials…from three different men. Bridger had ascertained my identity…he knew the Coyles were a venerable family…he knew of Altarbrook."

Hubert raised an imploring hand. "Please, Lizzie, you need not—"

"Bridger blackmailed my father," Lizzie said. "He claimed I had prostituted myself. This *man*…if one could refer to him thusly…he worked for the newspaper. Bridger told Father he would gather more stories from my *paramours*—the bastard's own word—and publish the entire sordid affair if we didn't comply with his demands. Over the past five years, the monetary strain imposed by that villain has grown severe."

I turned a wondering face on Hubert. "Your financial troubles."

Hubert lowered his gaze. He didn't need to confirm it.

I looked at Lizzie. "But that was five years ago, and it's no one's business but your own. I hardly see why your family should be held hostage by an avaricious fiend."

The Dismembered

Lizzie favored me with a mordant gaze. "Such concerns do appear trivial, given our current plight."

I closed my mouth, unable to contradict her.

Thirteen

We'd brooded in silence for several hours when we heard footfalls approaching. I joined Lizzie at the bars of our respective cells and listened with a mixture of dread and hope.

A familiar voice echoed down the gloomy corridor. "You down there, Mr. Coyle?"

Hubert sat up. "Tom?"

Mrs. Coyle staggered to her feet. "It's dear Mr. Erskine! Oh, Tom, do get us out of here."

Lizzie glanced at me, and some current of understanding passed between us. Like me, she did not seem to share her parents' faith in Tom Erskine. But we listened with interest as Violet said, "He killed Jimmy, Mr. Erskine."

"Aye," Erskine answered. "I saw the body laid out on the back lawn."

Hubert recoiled. "The back lawn?"

Erskine nodded. "I reckon Mr. Dunning believed my hounds could enjoy a snack."

Violet covered her mouth. "My God...you must tell them to retrieve his body, you can't let the—"

"I'm more concerned with *our* bodies," Lizzie interrupted. "How do you plan to get us out of here, Tom?"

Jonathan Janz

"Well, Miss Elizabeth," Erskine said, scratching his under-jaw, "I do have some ideas in that direction."

Hubert grasped the bars. "Have you the keys?"

"Mayhap I can get them," Erskine answered, "but to do so I'll need a little cooperation."

Mrs. Coyle frowned. "Cooperation?"

Erskine was silent a moment, a sly gleam in his eyes, then he limped toward Lizzie's cell and said, "Come closer, Miss Elizabeth."

She did as he bade. Erskine whispered something to Lizzie, and the next thing I knew, her hand flashed out between the bars and her fingernails raked down Erskine's face.

He sucked in air and stumbled back. "You vicious *cunt*! How dare you misuse me? I'm your only goddamned hope!"

Hubert stared at Lizzie in stupefaction. "Why on earth would you assault Tom?"

Lizzie nodded at Erskine. "Ask *him*."

Erskine's smile returned, only this time the harrowed troughs in his flesh lent it a sinister aura. "I merely asked the harlot if she'd suck me off. God knows she done enough whorin' when she moved to the city."

My hands knotted into fists. "If I find my way out of this cell, I promise I'll make you regret addressing a lady that way."

Erskine snorted. "*Lady*? Don't know what constitutes a lady in America, but in England, a lady don't open her legs for any bloke that passes by."

"And what of Sarah's promiscuity?" Lizzie asked.

Erskine leveled a forefinger at her. "Better watch yourself, Miss Elizabeth. Miss Sarah's gonna be the lady of this castle."

"It's quite alright, Tom," a voice called. "Lizzie has never given me the credit I deserve."

Smirking, Sarah approached us.

"You speak of *credit*?" Lizzie demanded. "You allowed our brother to be slain."

The Dismembered

Sarah moved past Tom. "Jimmy fell prey to his own debauchery. His life was forfeit years ago, the night he first tasted the demon absinthe."

Lizzie's eyes flashed. "You dare speak of demons? When you, like a mongrel dog, lap the blood of our brother from the rancid lips of your owner?"

Sarah's aloofness disappeared. "Richard is not my owner."

"Puppeteer then," Lizzie said, smiling savagely. "Do you honestly credit the tales about his mystical exploits? Do you believe you'll be rewarded for your calumny?"

"I already have," Sarah answered. "My throne awaits in the Great Hall, beside my true love."

Erskine nodded sagely. "Fashioned it out of a light-ning-struck yew, per Dunning's orders. Hell of a pain to locate, but once I found what I was looking for, I made one of the prettiest things you ever set eyes on." He turned a fond smile on Sarah. "Can't wait to see the lady gracing it."

"Soon, Tom," she said, taking one of his large hands in hers. "Soon."

They made to go.

"Mr. Erskine," I said.

Erskine directed a baleful stare my way. "What do you want?"

"Your hounds," I began. "Did you enjoy making monsters of them?"

"You'll not see them again, Mr. Pearce. Besides, they're gentle at heart."

"I've no doubt of that," I agreed. "Before your pernicious influence, I'm certain they were docile."

Erskine stared at me a long moment. "What's your damned point?"

I shrugged. "Only that you seem adept at coaxing the worst from others. How old was Sarah when you began offering her up to the Count for sexual pleasure?"

Sarah's mouth fell open, and Erskine's hand went to a bulge in his waistcoat.

Erskine showed his teeth. "You'd best not sass me again."

"Of course not," I agreed. "In delivering Sarah to the Count, you were only demonstrating your expertise in animal husbandry."

Lizzie laughed aloud, but Erskine and Sarah looked absolutely murderous. Erskine gripped the holstered firearm, his lips trembling. "Why you foul-mouthed little bastard."

"Don't, Tom," Sarah said. "Mr. Pearce will receive the ending he deserves." She linked her arm with Erskine's. "And we shall be present to witness it."

"You're right, Miss Sarah," Erskine said, as if from afar. "I'll enjoy watching you bleed, Pearce."

I bowed. "Watching is your specialty."

His lips formed into a snarl, but Sarah was already leading him away.

"Lewd old goblin," Lizzie remarked.

"He's been central to the entire scheme," I said. "His hounds are a safeguard, should we escape Castle Magnus."

Violet grunted. "Safeguard? What chance have we of ever leaving these cells, much less the castle?"

"Dunning plans on using us," I said, my chin resting on a crossbar. "There's little advantage to simply executing us, else he would have done so already."

"But use us how?" Hubert asked. His voice grew thick with emotion. "He's already taken Jimmy from me."

I glanced askance at him. "I'm sorry, Mr. Coyle. No parent should outlive his child."

"I wish I could hold your hand, Father," Lizzie said. "I know how you cherished him."

"I did." Hubert lowered his head. "I do." He gathered himself and looked at Lizzie. "I cherish each of you. And I'll die before allowing Richard Dunning to harm another member of my family."

The Dismembered

Though spoken with great conviction, I doubted the effectiveness of such a vow. We lapsed into moody silence. I ambled to the rear of my cell, sat down heavily, interlaced my fingers over my neck, and regarded the floor.

After a few minutes, Lizzie asked, "Do you want to talk about it?"

There was no point in pretending I didn't understand. "Not especially."

"When did you learn of your wife's infidelity?"

I laughed, but the sound was as joyless as a eulogy. "When I beheld her kissing a man on the dance floor."

She winced.

"We were out with a group of couples," I explained. "Angela had always been flirtatious, but I ascribed that to her vivacious personality. She was…playful. Full of life. When she left our table to waltz with another man, I didn't think anything of it. Not until I looked up and discovered their mouths locked together, his hands roving over her buttocks."

"That's terrible," Lizzie said.

"Yes. It was."

No one spoke for several minutes. Eventually, Lizzie broke the silence.

"After hearing of my degenerate behavior…," she said in a voice meant only for me.

"Yes?"

"Do you despise me?"

I chuckled. "Don't be absurd. We've all done things of which we aren't proud."

"Yes, but I—"

"Slept with men out of wedlock. And I was made the laughingstock of Boston. Which is worse?"

Another silence.

"Was it as awful as it sounds?" she asked.

"What, being cuckolded?"

Jonathan Janz

She waited.

"Worse than I ever would have dreamed," I answered. "Imagine all the trust you have, nested in one person. Imagine that person taking that trust and using it to betray you. Openly. Brazenly. With…" I took a breath, let it out. "…with the man you thought was your best friend."

"Oh, Arthur. I'm so sorry."

"Angela wasn't. Isn't. Will likely never be. I can't reconcile her behavior with the woman I married. I suppose people change."

"Can they change for the better as well?"

I turned to her, and in the wavering orange torchlight, I saw a woman without guile, without artifice. She was opening her heart to me, our plight perhaps galvanizing her to trust someone before her time on earth ended.

She searched my eyes. "Why did you come to England, Arthur?"

I hesitated, then decided on honesty. "I was approached by a private detective some months ago. He said he'd been employed by one of my father's colleagues and claimed to have information regarding his disappearance."

"Didn't that occur in your youth?"

"It did. But the mystery has plagued me since. Haunted me. When my father disappeared, my mother descended into sorrow. She endured for a few years, but in the end…she took her life."

Hubert said, "I'm sorry, Mr. Pearce."

"When the detective contacted me, I was dealing with Angela. But he was so persistent. He wouldn't quit until I agreed to hear him out. Once I had, the information was too compelling to ignore. I booked a voyage to London, and soon after, I met Sarah on the train."

Lizzie was frowning.

"What is it?" I asked.

The Dismembered

"Your train was bound for what county?"

"Shropshire," I answered. "Why?"

Footsteps interrupted her interrogation, but my curiosity had been piqued. "What are you thinking, Lizzie?"

She glanced at her father, who I noticed was gazing at me intently. "The Pearce name is no stranger to our area," she explained. "When the thought occurred to me earlier, I dismissed it as whimsy. But now…"

The footsteps grew louder, several sets of them.

I glanced from Lizzie to Hubert. "Would one of you please enlighten me? It's not as though we have a great deal of time."

Lizzie exchanged a look with her father. "One of the rumors about Count Dunning concerned an American named Pearce."

My heart thundered. The footfalls drew closer.

Hubert said, "His disappearance would have been around…1896?"

"1897," I said, dry-mouthed.

To our left, several figures began to materialize.

Lizzie bit her lower lip. "One of our servants told of a Mr. Pearce who'd stopped at the pub needing directions."

I closed my eyes. "Do I need to guess which servant?"

"Tom Erskine," Hubert said.

"And the destination my father was seeking?"

In a toneless voice, Lizzie answered, "Castle Magnus."

When I opened my eyes, figures were ranged before our cells. A score of them, far too many for us to overpower.

Leading the group was Mr. Broxton. "You ready to make history, my prancing little schoolmaster?"

Fourteen

J worried they'd chain our feet together or bind us with manacles. Instead, they surrounded us in a throng, prodding our bodies with sharp objects and taunting us as we labored up the stairs. Broxton was chief amongst our tormentors, but the gaunt-faced butler and the broad-shouldered maid also took great pleasure in jabbing us whenever we lagged.

As we trudged around and around the stone steps, I caught glimpses of the purpling dusk through the slender staircase windows. It would be full night soon, and I doubted I would ever again behold the sunlight or breathe the fragrant country air. These lugubrious thoughts were bound up with Lizzie, and I wondered passingly how our relationship might have developed had we not been embroiled in the Count's schemes. After the interminable climb, we found ourselves in the highest tower of Castle Magnus.

Mrs. Coyle uttered a shocked gasp, and Hubert whispered, "Oh my dear God."

The Western Tower was a carnival of depravity. There were naked corpses dangling from the vaulted conical ceiling, fifty of them at least, each one missing a different body part. I could only inspect the ghastly reliquary for a moment before horror overwhelmed me. Hubert and his wife clung to one another for comfort. Violet wept openly. Even Lizzie could not gaze upon the menagerie for long.

The tower floor was tiered, with three distinct elevations. We prisoners and our mob of captors stood on the lowest level. On the next level up, which rose perhaps six feet higher, several operating tables were arranged in a semi-circle, all pointing toward the uppermost elevation, where a dais was situated before the largest window in the castle. While the dais reminded me of an altar in some blasphemous church, it was the enormous stained glass window toward which the eye was drawn. This window was composed of multi-colored panes and featured a man and woman gazing ardently into one another's eyes. The woman was vaguely familiar, her beauty breathtaking.

The man, there could be no doubt, was Richard Dunning.

An idea began to form in the recesses of my mind. Before I could articulate it to Lizzie, however, the door behind us creaked open, and Count Dunning appeared. As one, the crowd of servants parted and bowed their heads.

Dunning strode forward and motioned toward the dais. "Magnificent, is it not? You are the first visitors to behold the majesty of the Western Tower."

"You killed all these people," Hubert said, eyeing the dangling corpses.

"Some," Dunning allowed. "I certainly performed procedures on them. Necessary trials in a grander pursuit."

Violet asked, "Why Sarah? Why not me?"

Lizzie shot a glance at her youngest sister. "Don't tell me you wish you'd been part of this monster's schemes?"

Violet shook her head. "Nothing on earth could make me participate in these accursed rites any longer. Yet…" She frowned. "…it's a bitter reality to be discarded. Particularly in favor of someone close to you."

The Dismembered

Her words caught me like a punch to the gut. I sensed Lizzie watching me.

Sarah Coyle, looking more icily beautiful than ever, stepped forward. "Where lies the mystery, Baby Sister? You're a plain-faced waif with the body of a prepubescent boy. Why settle for a table scrap when one can feast on a succulent steak?"

Tom Erskine bent double with laughter, and the Count grinned. "Well said, my Dearest Sarah. I've no doubt we could have made a life together."

Sarah's grin faded. "You mean we'll make one."

Something ruthless permeated the Count's gaze. "I mean what I said." He nodded at Broxton, who stalked forward and wrapped Sarah from behind in a bear hug.

Erskine's face twisted. "What the hell's the meaning of this?"

Dunning nodded. "McCray."

Another servant strode forward, a ginger-haired man of early middle age with a compact frame and an expressionless face. He seized one of Erskine's arms and bent it behind his back. Erskine pawed for his firearm, but in a trice McCray had it out of the holster and pressed against Erskine's temple.

"Gimme my gun and take your fuckin' hands off," Erskine growled. "So help me, I'll break your goddamned skull for you."

Hubert stepped forward. "Tell your man to release Sarah, Mr. Dunning."

The bull-shouldered maid smirked. "This ain't Altarbrook, Coyle. You don't tell my master what he should or shouldn't do."

Dunning approached the struggling Sarah. "Quite right, Miss Nichols. But you do broach an important subject."

"I do, sir?" Miss Nichols said, her eyebrows knitting.

"Indeed," Dunning answered, standing directly before Sarah.

She tried a smile. "What's the meaning of this, my love? Surely you've been deceived."

Dunning's eyes widened. "You dare speak of deception?"

"Tell me then," Sarah pleaded. "You know I worship you, Richard. You've revealed wonders I never dreamed possible."

"You've seen much, that is true," he agreed. "Yet you never understood my suffering."

Sarah opened her mouth to respond, but Broxton gave her a rough shake. "I've heard enough outa you, princess. 'Twas bad enough having to listen to your prattle on that train."

I made no move toward Broxton, for I was afraid of being similarly restrained, but I spoke loudly enough for him to hear me. "Actor, vintner. Something tells me your true profession lies elsewhere, Mr. Broxton."

He nodded. "The first sane words you've uttered, Pearce. I'm a taxidermist by trade."

"And it's time to prepare your next specimen," Dunning said. He nodded at McCray. The ginger-haired man wrestled Erskine forward until the older man lay facedown on a white operating table.

Dunning turned. "Maximov."

The gaunt butler strode forward and joined McCray in rolling Tom Erskine onto his back and binding his hands and feet with leather straps.

"I'll have your all your asses!" Erskine shouted, eliciting a chorus of laughter from the servants. Erskine glowered at them. "Go on, you piss pots. I'll feed you to my hounds."

Dunning said, "Broxton, would you provide Mr. Erskine with a companion?"

"Gladly, sir," Broxton answered. He lifted Sarah as easily as a child's doll, and though she spat curses, he soon had her strapped onto the table next to Erskine.

"Miss Nichols," Dunning said, "would you please prepare them?"

On cue the Irish maid moved to where Erskine and Sarah lay, produced a fillet knife, and began the job of scything through their clothing.

The Dismembered

This proved too much for Hubert. "Let her go!" he shouted.

I'd been so enraged with Sarah that I'd almost forgotten she was still Hubert's daughter. He broke from the group of servants and made it halfway up the steps before a pair of men fell on him and dragged him back.

"Don't hurt her!" Hubert shouted. "Don't take another of my children from me!"

Dunning favored him with a pitiless stare. "She ceased being your child long ago."

Miss Nichols worked steadily until both Erskine and Sarah lay naked within their leather bonds.

Whey-faced, Violet averted her eyes. "I can't bear this."

Dunning ignored her. "Dr. Crawley?"

A wizened little man detached himself from the crowd and made his way to the second tier. He carried a black bag, the sight of which chilled me to the marrow.

In a high, cultured voice, Dr. Crawley asked, "Which one first, sir?"

"Sarah," Dunning answered. "Since nothing is salvageable from Mr. Erskine, I think Broxton might as well tend to him straightaway."

Broxton's eyes broadened with pleasure, his yellow teeth gleaming within the tangled nest of beard. "It would please me greatly, sir."

Broxton produced a Bowie knife.

Erskine's eyes flew wide. "Now don't you—"

Before he could finish, the giant taxidermist plunged the blade into Erskine's breastbone and ripped him open all the way to the navel.

I turned away, sickened. I heard someone gagging, but the sound was drowned out by Erskine's inhuman shrieks and the cheering of Dunning's worshippers. I surveyed their mad faces, wondered dimly what Dunning might have promised them to secure such fanatical loyalty.

Jonathan Janz

"How can such things happen, Arthur?" Lizzie murmured. I peered into her eyes, wishing I had an answer. She looked as lost as I felt. This brutality was beyond imagining.

When Erskine's screams finally ended, Hubert and his wife implored Dunning to spare Sarah.

"And what will you offer?" Dunning asked.

"Take me instead," Hubert said.

"Or me," Mrs. Coyle added.

Sarah had swiveled her head on the table and was gazing, bleary-eyed, at her parents. "I'm so sorry," she said. "I never should have strayed."

Dunning smiled. "Ah, but stray you did, my dear.

"I thought we were to be together," she said in a small voice.

He loomed over her, stroked her hair. "We will, dear. In a sense."

Dr. Crawley shuffled up beside Dunning and asked, "Your wishes, sir?"

Dunning's eyes traveled down Sarah's body. "You know, Sarah, I must pay you a compliment. All these long years, I have lain with women in the vain hope that one of them would demonstrate the same anatomical compatibility as my Charlotte did."

"Charlotte?" Sarah asked.

Beside me, Lizzie sucked in breath, but before I could ask her why, Dunning continued. "The face was easy," he said. "So was the missing hand." He motioned toward Violet.

Sarah's expression was difficult to behold, a combination of bewilderment and hurt. "You told me the experiments were over."

"They are."

"But why then..." She nodded heavenward to indicate the mutilated bodies. "You only need two hands, two feet. Why all this butchery?"

He spread his arms as if it were obvious. "You said so yourself, Sarah. Experimentation. I always knew from which two

The Dismembered

families I would take my final ingredients, but I had to be certain the procedure would be successful. Hence my use of prostitutes and runaways. In the meantime, I have scoured the globe in search of the knowledge to bring my Charlotte back."

Hubert shook his head. "Confound it, man, who the devil is Charlotte?"

Dunning turned a countenance on Hubert that sent chills racing up and down my spine. "Fitting you should ask that, Mr. Coyle. Being descended from devils yourself."

He stalked toward Hubert. To me the Count had never looked more dangerous. Thunderheads threatened in his wide brow, the piercing brown eyes red-rimmed and wide. When he spoke, his bleach-white teeth flashed like terrible semaphores, their message a herald of anguish and death.

"'To love and be loved by me.' You no doubt recognize those words, Mr. Pearce?"

"Poe's 'Annabel Lee,'" I answered at once. "A fine piece of writing, though you corrupt it with your forked tongue."

Dunning grinned. "I'm a monster to you, but to Charlotte I was the sun and moon." He began to pace. "I was but a lowly carpenter's apprentice. Born to an unwed mother, my father a useless vagabond, I possessed none of the advantages with which you—" A disdainful glance at Hubert. "—have been gifted. My future appeared bleak...until I met Charlotte. My master, a decent man, had been contracted to perform repairs on Altarbrook."

Hubert and his wife exchanged an amazed look.

Dunning laced his hands behind his back and stepped onto the first platform. "Altarbrook. Even then it was the pride of the county. An ode to English morals. A testament to good loving." His lip curled. "A paean to the privileges of the rich."

Dunning said, "Dr. Crawley, please administer the anesthetic."

Crawley produced a hypodermic needle and injected Sarah's forearm. Hubert and Juniper Coyle were shouting at

Crawley to stop, but the doctor completed his task, and soon Sarah appeared to be sleeping soundly.

Dunning continued. "When I first beheld Charlotte she was reposing in the library, reading a Marlowe play. You see, she was a guest at Altarbrook, not a resident." The snarl reappeared. "Not a Coyle."

He nodded. "When I beheld her ethereal form…the delicate lines of her nose and lips…I knew I had found my purpose, knew that no barriers, societal or otherwise, would swerve me from attaining Charlotte's hand in marriage."

His eyes went steely. "She was, of course, promised to another."

He glowered at Hubert. "Your kind perpetuates the worst form of prejudice. Not only do you regard others as subhuman, you assure your offspring will remain pure by selling them off to other greedmongers."

The Count paced the platform, every eye in the room riveted on his magnetic form. "Charlotte, thank the stars, cared nothing for social class, cared even less about Thomas Coyle, the indolent lout to whom she'd been promised."

Dunning stopped, gazed up at the stained glass window, the colors of which glinted in the electric chandelier glow. "We fell irretrievably in love. We spent months in each other's arms, unbeknownst to her idiot fiancé." His voice went lower, a rawness bleeding into its tones. "She was forced to marry. And Thomas…he demanded she…he forced her to consummate the infernal union. And when it was over, he knew something was amiss…knew he wasn't her first lover. He railed at her, ill-treated her, until she admitted the truth."

Dunning faced us, his handsome visage hideous to behold. "The families were disgraced, or believed they would be. They agreed on a drastic solution. A party was dispatched to my employer, the carpenter's home. I was living in their attic. The patriarchs of both families doused the exterior of the wooden

The Dismembered

dwelling with kerosene. I am told Thomas himself used his torch to ignite the blaze." Dunning's gaze became unfocused, as though he were replaying the terrible night in his mind. "The first floor went up immediately. The carpenter, his wife, his two young sons...all lost. I too would have perished had not a figure, undetected by the others, stolen to the rear of the dwelling, scaled an old elm tree to the second floor, and used the attic ladder to reach me."

I was gripped with a sense of crawling dread. Though it was easy to regard the Count as a demon, the tale he was recounting had the effect of humanizing him, of engendering in me a curiosity of what he might have become had he and Charlotte been allowed to live as husband and wife.

He swallowed, his voice grown thick with emotion. "Charlotte roused me from my slumber. She was already coughing. So was I. Selflessly, she dragged my convulsed body toward the only means of egress, a vented area in the attic gable through which I had often gazed when my longing for Charlotte forbade sleep. The conflagration intensifying beneath us, she kicked out the wooden vent slats, and trusting providence to preserve me, she shoved me bodily through the opening."

The Count took in a shuddering breath. "I was lucky. The shrubs massed against the house—yew bushes, it turned out—broke my fall. Charlotte was not so lucky. Before she could follow me, the attic floor gave way. She..." His chest hitched. "...she was burned." Dunning looked up at us. "But not killed."

He stepped onto the highest platform, the dais equipped with two operating tables. I noticed cables drooping from one table to the other. Though my eye had been drawn toward the stained-glass images of Dunning and his beloved Charlotte, I now marked the presence of electrical equipment on the far edge of the dais, equipment that seemed to be connected to the operating tables.

Dunning sighed. "They thought she was dead. Though overcome with smoke, I charged back into the house and found

Charlotte lying broken on the floor. Her body was badly charred, her face unrecognizable. But yet…she lived. Somehow, I know not how, I found a way out of the inferno. When I emerged from the blaze bearing her body, I collapsed, overcome by smoke inhalation. Some members of the hateful mob must have been moved to compassion by the devotion between me and my love, and I was spared. Charlotte awakened, though she now dwelled in a nightmare world of agony and disfigurement."

Dunning glowered at Mr. and Mrs. Coyle. "Your ancestors wanted nothing to do with Charlotte now that she bore the scars of the inferno. Thomas, of course, sought a divorce, but rather than admit the truth—that he could no longer bear to look upon the altered countenance of his bride—he humiliated her by making public her infidelity. The divorce was finalized while she languished in a London hospital.

"After months of torment and ineffective surgeries, it became apparent that recovery was not feasible. Because I loved her as much as ever, I had her brought to a plot of land I had inherited." An ironic smile. "It seems the carpenter cared for me more than I'd realized, and had included a stipulation in his will that, were any calamity to befall his wife and children, I would become his heir."

The Count raised his arms. "This land is the site of the carpenter's old home. The money he'd saved allowed me to build another dwelling, which can still be found on the southern corner of the property."

Dunning glanced at Lizzie. "You've come the nearest, I think, to solving the mystery of my age. Care to guess?"

"You built this castle," she said.

"Ah," he answered, eyes alight.

"But that's not possible," Mrs. Coyle said. "Castle Magnus was constructed only a century after Altarbrook, and our home is nearly three hundred years old."

"Good God," Hubert muttered. "But how did you become so wealthy?"

The Dismembered

The Count lowered his nose at Hubert. "Singlemindedness. While I gradually amassed my fortune, I traveled the world to find substances purported to possess restorative powers. China. Mongolia. The Carpathian Mountains. And as I've canvassed the globe, I've never forgotten those two glorious years Charlotte and I spent together."

Noticing our surprise, Dunning nodded. "That's right. For two years, Charlotte lived with me in my humble dwelling. I attended to her every need, read her poetry, and, when she was able, carried her outside to breathe the fresh air. She was perpetually in pain, no matter what remedies I attempted, but I believe she was happy. She knew I cared nothing of her scars, or her blindness. All that mattered was that we were together."

His voice sank to nearly a whisper. "At the end of two years, she slipped away. Though I mourned her, I knew that death was not the end. I had already read much of the afterlife, of the possibility of resurrection. You see, it all comes down to the communion between the flesh and the invisible powers that surround us."

His manner grew animated. "It has taken me centuries, but I have finally perfected the process. Thankfully, the Coyle family still resides in its sanctuary of prejudice and leisure."

I'm afraid I gasped aloud.

"This Charlotte," I said, "the one who was taken from you."

Dunning's gaze was eager. "Yes?"

"What was her maiden name?"

Dunning grinned. "Your father suspected it too."

"Don't talk of my father."

"He was easy to lure to Castle Magnus. A genealogist attempting to solve the mystery of his own heritage..."

I bit down on my retort, gone dumb with outrage.

"That's right," Dunning said. "Charlotte's maiden name was Pearce."

Fifteen

"But that means...," I started, gazing up at the mutilated corpses.

"Over there," Dunning said, indicating a body to my right.

I didn't want to gaze into my father's dead face, but I had to know what had become of him.

Dunning said, "The headless one."

The body could have been any man in the prime of his life, but somehow I knew Dunning was telling the truth. The leathery body belonged to my father.

Lizzie took my hand in both of hers. "I'm sorry, Arthur."

"You've no doubt guessed that it was I who hired the detective that contacted you," Dunning said. "And you proved as foolishly emotional as your father."

I drew in a shuddering breath and did my best to retain my composure. It was difficult though. Memories of my dad roughhousing with me when I was a boy kept intruding.

Dunning nodded at our group. "Bind them."

I was jerked away from Lizzie. Though we resisted, the five of us were soon strapped on our respective tables on the first platform. I noted with misgiving the two operating tables on the uppermost dais, though from my vantage point I could not see what, if anything, lay on their white surfaces.

"Dr. Crawley," Dunning said. "Please perform the procedure."

Hubert and Juniper Coyle began to wail, but I could only look away, my eyes closed tight against the carnage occurring on the operating table next to mine.

As Dr. Crawley sawed through Sarah Coyle's flesh and bones, I found myself retreating into the haven of early childhood memories. My father exhorting me to tell him a scary story. My mother, who possessed an affinity for the macabre, reading excerpts of "The Raven" while our warm Boston hearth flickered and danced. I remembered a time when my father returned home deflated, his funding at Harvard having been reduced. "Genealogy," I remembered him saying, "isn't a priority for the university. Every penny is allocated to industrialization. We destroy the present while forgetting the past." I remembered hugging my father, telling him genealogy was important to me, though I couldn't at the time pronounce the word. Father carrying me to bed…smiling down at me, telling me we'd be fine… telling me he was proud of me…

Lizzie's voice recalled me to our present plight: "Look at me, Arthur."

I did not want to open my eyes, but her voice punctured the protective dome with which I'd girded my sanity. I met her gaze.

"We need to think," she said in a low voice, one I could scarcely make out beneath the sobs of her family members and the execrable noises issuing from the operating table. "We need to devise a plan."

There was determination in her eyes, and I yearned to muster some of my own. But the depravity we were witnessing resonated in my mind, muddying my thoughts and sending my nerves into an apoplectic frenzy.

"Arthur," she persisted. "Look into my eyes."

I did and found that focusing on her profound blue gaze was a means of escaping, if only for a moment, the horror of Sarah's vivisection.

The Dismembered

Lizzie nodded. "We need to find a way of hurting Dunning. Only by aiming at the head of the beast will the body be neutralized."

I swallowed the sick lump in my throat. Her words were penetrating the fog of terror. If Dunning were killed or incapacitated, his servants would become aimless. They worshiped Dunning and assumed he would never be challenged.

But how to challenge him?

A murmur rippled through the crowd, and when I turned to see what it was that had transfixed them, I beheld the most repellant vision imaginable.

His amputation completed, Dr. Crawley lifted Sarah Coyle's midsection—severed neatly at the thighs and above the hipbones—and bore it up the stairs to the uppermost dais. When I saw the needle begin to rise and fall from his wrinkled grip, I realized what was on one of the tables. I imagined Sarah Coyle's abdomen...Violet Coyle's hand...the other body parts Dunning had harvested and preserved...

Broxton wore a sullen frown. "Coulda done that myself," he grumbled. "No need for this doddering old fool."

Something Dunning had said recurred to me. I craned my head off the table to find him peering at me from the uppermost platform. "Your writer's mind is at work," Dunning said. "I can see it in your eyes."

Ignoring the incessant rise and fall of Crawley's needle, I said, "You harvested most of your...your *creation* from prostitutes and runaways."

Pride showed in his sadistic visage. "I did."

"That means you've already completed most of the..."

"The body," he finished.

I cleared my throat, my gag reflex having been triggered by the notion of a patchwork corpse.

"You told us the face was easy," I said.

Dunning regarded me blandly. "So I did."

Jonathan Janz

I waited, not wanting to hear the answer but knowing what it would be just the same.

Dunning glanced at his henchmen. "Please prepare Miss Elizabeth for surgery."

And as Dr. Crawley reached into his bag and came out with a scalpel, Lizzie began to scream.

Part THREE

Inferno

Sixteen

"You mustn't hurt Lizzie," Violet pleaded.

I glanced at Sarah's ruined body, the legs severed at the thighs, the torso terminating just below the navel. Blood and entrails were strewn about the table. The sight made my stomach clench.

"Have you no heart?" Hubert implored.

"Of course I do," Dunning answered. "I harvested it from a Parisian whore last winter."

Crawley finished his sewing, made his way down the steps to the lower platform, and retrieved his bone saw.

The hideous possibility that Lizzie, too, might become one of Dunning's victims galvanized me into speech. "Do you truly believe Charlotte would have approved of this?"

Dunning grew still. His expression was impossible to interpret, but it was obvious I had broken through his insouciant veneer. He motioned toward his servants. "Broxton. McCray. Maximov. Have Miss Elizabeth and Mr. Pearce moved to the altar."

The altar.

I shivered. It was one thing to rob graves, to harvest parts from dead bodies. But *this*...I gazed up at the dangling bodies, which exhibited various forms of mutilation…this was the nadir of evil.

Dunning's men grasped my table, lifted it into the air. The jostling motion sent my pulse racing, but not nearly as much as the sight of Lizzie being borne aloft beside me.

"Be careful," Dunning instructed as his servants bore our tables toward the uppermost platform. "Mind the wires, men."

Lizzie's table came to rest between the equipment and one of the tables. I caught a glimpse of the shriveled, pathetic form lying on that table and wondered if Charlotte Pearce could have guessed where her body might someday end up. Though mummified, the skin sunken and darkened to a dusty umber shade, I could still make out the caul of scar tissue that had covered the poor woman's face and most of her body. I remembered her devotion to Dunning, the sacrifice she'd made. I couldn't help but remember Dunning too, who at one time wasn't a blood-thirsty fiend. Who had loved a woman as I had once loved Angela…and was beginning to love Lizzie.

I sighed, wishing Lizzie and I had met under different circumstances. I caught her gazing at me from her table, the leather straps binding her limbs but allowing her head to move. Her eyes yet retained that spark of hope, that fierce determination. I wondered if Charlotte's eyes had reflected the same grimness, the same resolve. Perhaps Dunning could relate to the desire to preserve what we love. In his own way, I supposed he understood it better than anyone.

I looked at what lay on the table beside me, and all charitable thoughts about Dunning were engulfed in a sheet of horrified flame.

The figure on the table had been harvested from victims beyond counting. The toes of each foot had been stitched on, the feet sutured to the ankles. Fresh blood seeped from the ragged fissures where Sarah's thighs had been attached to the legs.

The fleshless cavity of a raven-tressed head glistened.

The Dismembered

Dunning noticed my aghast expression. "Charlotte's new shell presents a disconcerting picture. However, when the eternal essence of my beloved is channeled into the dead flesh, the stitches you see, the imperfections, will all blend into a glorious sameness, perfect in their unification and impervious to earthly complications."

Seeing the question in my face, Dunning went on. "There is yet no formula for eternal life, Mr. Pearce. True, I have overmastered disease, sickness, even the more extraordinary traumas that undo common men. There are a handful of us—Rasputin, the Antonov Sisters, a group of actors led by a man named Price—who have pioneered methods of surviving famine, gunshot wounds, drowning." A glance at the shriveled corpse of Charlotte Pearce. "Even fire."

Dunning shook his head. "But hardiness, durability, these are not the same as immortality." He reached out, caressed the dark hair of the faceless patchwork corpse. "Until now."

Lizzie said, "Immortality is a dream."

At Lizzie's words, my trance broke. "What if you're successful? What if you revive Charlotte? Assuming she accepts what you've done to her…assuming this accursed 'shell' as you call it transforms into something that doesn't vex the eyes…assuming she prefers her new physical form to her old, despite the fact that you're giving her an entirely different face than the one with whom you fell in love…assuming all these things, won't you still be susceptible to mortal perils? Wouldn't it be a bitter irony if she were granted eternal life while you passed on to the Underworld?"

I thought my words would enrage him, but he merely chuckled. "Charlotte has not been dormant these many years, Mr. Pearce. I'm surprised you'd make such an assumption."

Lizzie raised her head. "You believe Charlotte is aware of all this? That she's—" Lizzie glanced at the shriveled twist of mummy lying beside her, "—that this *thing* can hear us?"

A touch of asperity sounded in Dunning's voice. "This *thing* is a portion of Charlotte's essential being. It's why her earthly body must be part of this ceremony. Without her blood…"

The sardonic glint in Lizzie's eyes returned. "Then is she listening to us now, inside this wrinkled piece of cowhide?"

"Your attempts at baiting me are as transparent as they are ineffectual, Miss Elizabeth. But that face of yours…it is indescribably lovely." He nodded. "Dr. Crawley."

Crawley strode forward, the scalpel poised before him.

"Wait," I said. I nodded at the monstrosity next to me, the hollowed-out facial cavity framed by lustrous black hair. "You cannot simply stretch Lizzie's face over that…void." I swallowed, feeling like a lunatic for discussing such matters. "There has to be—"

"A brain," Dunning finished. "Quite right, Mr. Pearce. Quite right."

Oh no, I thought.

"Don't touch him!" Lizzie shouted.

"The brain is a complex object," Dunning mused. "I think it might be easier if the head were removed first." He motioned to someone on the lower platform. "Mr. Broxton here has suffered an injury at your hands, Mr. Pearce. I think he would appreciate some recompense."

Broxton's ursine form clumped up the steps. "You're goddamned right I would."

I watched in dread as Dr. Crawley offered Broxton the bloody bone saw that had been used on Sarah Coyle. "Nothing to it," Crawley said.

"I know there ain't," Broxton growled. He yanked the bone saw out of Crawley's hand. "I'm gonna enjoy this." He stalked toward me.

The Coyles were shouting for Broxton to stop. The servants responded with a chorus of taunts. Fear bloomed in Lizzie's eyes. Crawley made his way around her table, reached for her, but she thrashed her head to avoid his grasp.

The Dismembered

"Maximov," Dunning called.

Maximov broke from the crowd, the gaunt butler eager to participate.

Dunning nodded. "McCray, you remain and give us aid. Miss Nichols, you and the rest take the other Coyles outside. We have no need of them anymore."

Miss Nichols's grin was ghastly. "What shall we do with them, my Lord?"

Dunning winked. "Mr. Erskine's hounds deserve a repast, I think."

Cheers erupted from the crowd as Violet and her parents were dragged away.

Maximov reached Lizzie's table. He grasped her head roughly, and Crawley brought the scalpel toward her face.

"They're doing it wrong," I said.

The bone saw clutched in one big paw, Broxton glared down at me. "What the fuck are you on about?"

"The incision," I said, nodding toward Lizzie. "The scalpel is too far from her hairline."

Broxton scowled. "What's that got to do—"

"As a taxidermist you must understand the importance of precision. An excess of skin can always be excised, but if Crawley leaves too little..." I let the thought sink in. I only hoped Broxton's mind worked quickly enough. The scalpel was nearly touching Lizzie's flesh.

Broxton snapped at Crawley. "Not so low, damn you. Cut 'er along the hairline."

Crawley froze, the scalpel pressing Lizzie's flesh. I watched in numb horror as a slender rivulet of blood trickled down her temple.

Now, I thought. *Now or never, damn you!*

Though my leather bonds forbade much movement, I was yet able to work a hand into my hip pocket and retrieve the steak knife. My tongue poking out the corner of my mouth, I began sawing into the leather strap binding my arms to the table. It was an awkward angle, but the knife was sharp. I heard the leather parting a little at a time.

"Don't tell me my business," Crawley snapped.

But Broxton's ire was greater. "You'll not spoil the master's work, Crawley, not at this late hour."

"Gentlemen," Dunning said. "We must maintain our focus." With this, He moved over to the control center and switched on his mechanisms. The noises that issued from the machines, which in size reminded me of wood-burning stoves, hummed and throbbed, but they could not drown out the growing antagonism between Crawley and Broxton.

"There's plenty of skin here," Crawley argued. "We don't want Miss Charlotte's face to be baggy."

"It ain't gonna be *baggy*," Broxton said, "it's gonna be so tight she won't be able to do aught but stare."

I had almost sawn through the leather strap.

Lizzie's eyes kept shifting from Crawley to Broxton, and occasionally to Maximov, who clutched her by the temples.

The strap parted.

My first instinct was to leap to my feet, but of course that was impossible because the second leather strap still pinned down my legs. I raised my head and saw that the buckle holding the strap in place was positioned directly between my feet. To unfasten it, I'd have to sit up, and at that point the others would know I was loose. With a quick glance I noted that Dunning was engaged with his machinery, that Maximov and McCray were listening to Crawley and Broxton argue.

I decided I had no choice. They would never be more distracted than they were now.

I sat up, but I did so as gradually as I could, so as not to attract attention. I dared not look behind me to see if McCray had marked my movements. The only sounds I heard were the throb of Dunning's machinery and the curses Broxton and Crawley were hurling at each other. I reached down, unfastened

The Dismembered

the leather strap. The buckle came loose quietly, the strap whispering over my shins. My relief was exquisite.

But Lizzie's life hung in the balance.

I slid my legs over the side of the table and faced the arguing men.

A gloating Irish voice said, "Did the little Yankee piglet get loose?"

I faced McCray. "Watching all this butchery made me feel excluded. I want to know how it feels."

And before he could respond, I plunged the knife into his belly.

Seventeen

aping, McCray fell against me.

"So that's how it feels," I said.

McCray's body slithered downward, the blood spurting from the wound in his belly. The others gaped at us. Lizzie's eyes were wild with excitement. Broxton and Maximov stared at McCray's writhing form without emotion. Crawley looked appalled. I could see in his rheumy eyes that the possibility of someone attacking Dunning's people had never occurred to him, so complete was his faith in the Count's supremacy.

Dunning himself was smiling as though he'd anticipated this turn of events. "I made a prudent decision in bringing you here, Mr. Pearce. Not only are you descended from Charlotte's line, you are possessed of a brilliant intellect, one whose work-ings remind me of my beloved."

His hands poised on the humming controls, he said, "Did you know I suspected you were related to Charlotte even before I learned you had penned that splendid novel?"

I listened to him with as much interest as I could muster, though it was difficult with McCray vomiting blood on my shoes.

Dunning went on. "Maximov keeps abreast of literary trends, not only so I'm aware of any salient piece of intelligence, but because he loves a good yarn."

Jonathan Janz

I glanced at Maximov, whose gaunt face was so cold I couldn't imagine him enjoying anything, much less a tale of fiction.

"He raved about one of your stories in *Pearson's*. I devoured it on the spot but didn't check the author's name until after I'd finished. Imagine my rapture at learning of your possible connection to my beloved! The Fates were clearly at work."

He spread his long arms. "Don't you see, Mr. Pearce? Charlotte used to tell stories as well, and in time, she would have become a renowned author. Her narrative voice was uncannily like yours, and that—" A reptilian grin, "—is why I must use your brain in her revivification."

I glanced at the shriveled mummy.

"Haven't you considered," Dunning went on, "that traces of your old self will coalesce with Charlotte's? That, in a singular manner, you will enjoy the benefits of eternal life as surely as will my beloved?"

The Count's words dizzied me. I had overcome McCray, but I'd utilized the element of surprise, which would no longer avail me. With Dunning, Maximov, Broxton, and even old Crawley on their guard—not to mention the legion of servants awaiting at the base of the castle—I hardly stood a chance.

I looked at Lizzie, who was watching me intently. Her eyes kept flicking to something, signaling me in some way. I followed her gaze and discovered what she was indicating. Moreover, I realized what I had to do.

I smiled. Leave it to Lizzie to lead me through the darkness.

"There will be no resurrection," I said.

Dunning's grin never wavered. "You are powerless to prevent it."

"Am I?" I asked, and before one of his henchmen could stop me, I reached down and scooped up the patchwork body from the table.

"*What are you doing?*" Dunning gasped.

"Manumitting us from your accursed schemes," I said.

The Dismembered

I took a step toward the stained glass window, the stitched mannekin flopping in my arms.

"No!" he said, raising a hand.

I paused. "Let Lizzie go."

He grinned incredulously. "What will this *accomplish*, Mr. Pearce? The moment we've apprehended you, we'll simply bind Miss Elizabeth again."

"Fortunately," I said, "you're not bargaining from a position of strength."

Dunning's cruel smile thinned. "So be it. For now. Crawley?"

Crawley set the scalpel aside and unfastened the straps binding Lizzie.

Maximov and Broxton were creeping forward. I edged closer to the stained glass. "Don't move."

"Listen to him!" Dunning commanded.

The brutes stopped, looking eager to crush my bones.

"Let Lizzie leave the castle," I said.

Dunning chuckled. "I'm afraid that's not possible. You see, her face is the loveliest I've beheld since the night my Charlotte was burned."

"Then on one thing we agree." My eyes fixed on Lizzie's. "Whatever happens, I want you to know you were my ideal partner."

Despite our predicament, Lizzie managed to look pleased.

"In fact," I said, "you're far too magnificent to waste on this vile sack of body parts."

Dunning saw what I intended. "*Don't you dare—*" he began.

But it was too late. With all my strength, I pivoted and heaved the stitched body at the stained glass panes. The faceless head hit first, a halo of yellow glass shattering around it, then the entire body followed, splintering the window with arms and legs splayed, shards of red, green, yellow, and blue glittering in the tower lamps and winking out as they were devoured by the night. The stitched body tumbled gracefully from our view. Three stories below was an outcropping balcony, but the body merely struck its outer edge and continued its descent. We watched it fall until the darkness swallowed it up.

Then the Count turned to me.

Eighteen

Dunning's upper lip curled. "Do you really think you've beaten me?"

I kept silent. I had no more cards to play. Lizzie and I were down to our wiles and whatever strength we possessed.

Dunning moved toward me with slow, purposeful strides. "You think by casting that body out the window, you've accomplished anything? There might be a few broken bones to repair, some replacement parts to harvest, but—"

He broke off, his mouth opening in shock.

A violent snarling reached our ears.

Erskine's dogs had found the stitched body.

"I'll destroy you!" Dunning roared.

Had I not leapt aside, my life would have ended at that moment. The fury in Dunning's face surpassed any I had ever beheld. He smashed into the foot of an operating table, which toppled from the impact. Having dove to the left to avoid the Count's hurtling form, I found myself crowded against the legs of my own vacant table, which was the only obstacle between me, Maximov, and Broxton.

Without pause, I lunged toward my enemies, and in doing so overturned my table. Broxton was close enough to receive the brunt of its impact, the hard edge knocking against his thighs and driving him into the table on which rested Charlotte's mummified corpse. Broxton didn't topple, but because he was such an enormous man, the table and the corpse did.

I heard a gasp behind me, and then Dunning was thundering, "Restore her, Crawley! Restore her at once!"

I spun, meaning to retrieve the knife I'd embedded in McCray's belly, but that's when the Fates forsook me. Before I could start toward McCray's convulsing body, rough hands seized my shoulders.

Maximov swung. His cudgel fist battered my stomach with the full force of malice. I doubled over, the breath whooshing out of me, and before I could replace the air I'd lost, he was spinning me, jerking me upright to face Broxton, who was stomping toward me, a fist raised. Staring at that hand, which in magnitude resembled a holiday turkey, I wriggled in Maximov's grip, but the butler was much too strong. Broxton bore down on me, mouth twisted in a vicious grin.

Something darted toward him, and instead of delivering what undoubtedly would have been a debilitating blow, Broxton bellowed in pain.

Lizzie had plunged the scalpel into Broxton's side.

We stared at her in shock. Crawley's lips trembled in outrage. "Give me back my scalpel."

Lizzie's face was a mask of vengeance. I don't know whether she was thinking about Sarah or Jimmy or the manner in which we had been ill-used, but whatever the case, there was no hesitation in her lunge toward the doctor. Before the wizened ghoul could raise his hands, Lizzie had whipped the scalpel across his throat, opening it as easily as one would a paper parcel. The doctor's arterial blood sprayed Lizzie and Broxton.

Realizing Maximov's grip on my arms had slackened, I pumped an elbow into his ribcage. Maximov released me, but instead of turning on him, I went for Charlotte's corpse. If I

The Dismembered

could cast her pathetic remains through the shattered window and consign them to the hounds, I might put an end to Dunning's deranged fantasy of resurrecting her.

But Dunning was swifter.

He caught me from behind, lifted me. "Your mind is sharp, Mr. Pearce, but you forget my experience. I know your thoughts before you do."

"But do you know mine?" Lizzie demanded.

The Count whirled, jerking me with him, and I discovered Lizzie had saved me again. She'd stolen over to Charlotte's mummy and grasped it by the shoulders, the eyeless sockets gaping at us, the open mouth fixed in a silent shriek. The desiccated face evoked pity in me, even under these bizarre circumstances.

Dunning dropped me so suddenly I barely had time to catch myself. Through clenched teeth he growled, "*Put...her...down.*"

"Let us go," Lizzie demanded. She stood three feet from the open window, ready to cast the corpse into the night. I didn't know if Erskine's hounds would take to Charlotte's bloodless body the way they had the stitched monstrosity, but it was evident that the Count was unwilling to risk that chance.

Dunning's mouth split in a cunning grin. "Fine. I will give you a head start. Put her down, and I'll allow you to reach the door before we follow."

"That's not enough," I said. "Let us escape Castle Magnus. Lizzie's parents and little sister as well."

Dunning laughed.

"You've made your decision then?" Lizzie asked.

Dunning wiped away a mirthful tear. "My dear, there's no decision to make. Your lives have come to an end. It's time for my beloved to join me in the existence we both deserve."

Lizzie nodded. "What you deserve."

The Count must have realized what she intended, for he was already leaping forward as Lizzie thrust the corpse toward the window. One moment Charlotte's mummy was disappearing through the aperture; the next, Dunning's tenebrous form was following.

We all stood gaping as the Count plummeted into the night.

Bellowing with outrage, Maximov lunged at Lizzie, his wiry body crashing into her and smashing her into the wall below the shattered window.

I lunged at Maximov, but as I did, he gained his feet and spun toward me. I thought Lizzie had been knocked unconscious by Maximov's brutal tackle, but as I had so many times, I realized I'd underestimated her.

Maximov bellowed in pain and reached down to seize the scalpel, which Lizzie had buried in his calf. I tore down at Maximov, who was in the process of extricating the scalpel. The punch caught the Russian in the forehead. Maximov staggered. He turned to me, fists raised, but before he could swing, his face contorted again.

Lizzie had taken hold of the scalpel handle, was driving it deeper into his calf.

I swung, felt his teeth shatter under the force of my blow. Maximov stumbled back, his head smashing against the stone windowsill. Lizzie scrambled on top of him and began raining blows at his face. For the briefest moment I marveled at what a team Lizzie and I made.

"You haven't done a thing," a voice growled.

Broxton limped toward me, the blood from his side dark and gleaming in the torch light. He nodded. "Listen."

Not wanting to take my eyes off him for an instant, but sensing this was no trick, I followed his gaze and peered into the night. A voice called out from below.

Dunning.

At once, I understood how it had happened. The outcropping balcony three stories below had not caught the lifeless body I'd cast out the window, but Dunning—unspeakably virile and

The Dismembered

endowed with supernatural powers—had latched onto it before plummeting to his death.

"Help us!" Dunning commanded.

Broxton sneered with measureless hatred. "You're a dead man, Pearce. We'll have you and your stinking harlot before you get halfway down the stairs."

I'd taken a step toward Lizzie with the intention of prying her off Maximov—who lay insensate under her persistent blows—and escaping with her down the stairs. But fleeing was what Broxton assumed I would do.

And staring into his leering face, I realized that's what I'd been doing ever since the night I beheld my wife kissing another man.

Fleeing. Fleeing from embarrassment, fleeing from self-doubt. Fleeing from *life*.

Lizzie was watching me, her fists slick with blood, the beaten Russian unconscious beneath her. There was fire in her eyes.

I clenched my teeth.

I'd assumed my wife's betrayal was in some way precipitated by my behavior. It had taken Lizzie's ferocious goodness to waken me from my nightmare of self-loathing.

Broxton waggled his eyebrows at me. "Better run, little writer. Better run while you still got those horns to lead you."

I thought of Dunning on the balcony below us. I thought of Maximov, unconscious, sprawled at the base of the window. I thought of the fleeting moments we had to escape this hellish predicament.

Then I thought of Lizzie's fighting spirit and knew what I had to do.

I swung at Broxton's leering face.

He caught my fist and squeezed. Wincing, I kicked him in the groin.

Broxton doubled up, and when he did, I shot up a knee, nailed him between the eyes. His head snapped up, and then I was firing blows at him, my arms a flurry of motion. I didn't have Broxton's girth, but I'd always kept my muscles in good trim, my body stronger than the average man. Even if I was only a writer.

Broxton went stumbling away, one arm frozen in a warding off gesture. He was muttering curses, attempting to regain his footing, but I was possessed, the frustration of the past gushing into my blows. I smashed him with a violent right fist to the ear. He yelped. I cut loose with a left-handed jab to the jaw. His teeth clicked together, and from the shrill cry he emitted and the sudden spurt of blood that slopped over his bottom lip, I knew he'd bitten down on his tongue, perhaps severing it.

Lizzie had retrieved a shard of windowpane and was stalking toward the recovering Maximov. She was as merciless as she was resilient. Blood dripped from her fingers. Sweat streamed from her brow. Her clothing was ripped and stained.

Never had I so yearned to kiss her.

But Broxton was lumbering toward me. He looked terrible, but beneath the pain and the blood, there was a seething rage. His fist hit me in the chest, and though the blow was a powerful one, it wasn't enough to deter me. I planted my feet, cocked my fist, and returned the favor, only instead of his chest, I aimed for his nose.

And connected.

As his head snapped back and his mouth unhinged in a strident roar, I saw the terror in his eyes. He was right to be frightened.

As I followed his stumbling body toward Dunning's machinery, I glanced at Lizzie, who at that moment plunged the wicked shard of glass into Maximov's throat. Blood sprayed everywhere. A bit lightheaded, I shifted my attention to Broxton.

Though time was short, and Dunning would soon be pursuing us again, I knew what I had to do. Broxton had landed on the control panel of Dunning's blasphemous machinery, which hummed and crackled as though eager to inject its demented energy into some new host. When I'd ripped the corpse of

The Dismembered

Dunning's beloved from the table, I'd detached the cables that had linked her to the machine. Now I reached down and seized the connecting mechanism, which turned out to be a simple steel clamp. I spun toward Broxton, who raised his arms to fend me off. But he need not have worried. It wasn't his face I sought.

I darted in, attached the clamp to his groin, and yanked down on a red lever.

Broxton jittered, his arms jagging like he was performing some trendy new dance. The commingled odors of burning fabric and scorched skin reached my nostrils. The huge man lolled sideways and jerked in his death throes.

I turned from the dying taxidermist and saw Lizzie rise, the front of her dress glistening with blood. Her eyes gleamed.

"We have to save Violet and my parents," she said.

I nodded.

Froze.

She had taken several strides toward the door, but now paused and stared at me. "What is it, Arthur? We have to go!"

"We'll be running into a mob…"

The steel returned to her eyes. "We can't leave my family."

"We aren't leaving anyone," I answered. "But we aren't racing toward death either."

"Then…" She frowned. "Arthur, what are you doing with that bone saw?"

"Look away if you want," I said, going to work.

She didn't. Instead, she witnessed the brief but gruesome act.

Returning to her I said, "Dunning must have been injured in that fall. He fell three stories onto hard stone."

Her eyes never left what my fingers grasped. "Do you think that will—"

"I don't know," I said. "But it's the only idea I have."

She seemed to consider. Then she hustled over to the machinery, which was smoking and sparking. She removed the clamp from Broxton's crotch and attached it to a baize curtain. In short order, the curtain caught fire. Soon, a nearby tapestry began to flicker as well.

Lizzie returned to me, and together, we dashed toward the stairwell.

Nineteen

We were rounding the spiral staircase when Lizzie shot me a fearful look. "Do you think they're alive?"

I didn't answer. We both understood the chances of her family surviving the mob of servants were minimal. We clattered down the stairs, and as we neared the door from which I believed Dunning would any moment emerge, that primitive sense of terror returned. My flesh tightened into goosebumps, the tiny hairs on my neck standing up. If Dunning believed his beloved Charlotte was safe, and he'd incurred no major injuries himself, he might already be waiting for us in the stairwell.

Or might come bursting out the doorway I beheld.

"Is that where—" Lizzie began, but I nodded, hastened our descent to nearly a sprint. We were in danger of tumbling headlong down the staircase, but that, I judged, would be preferable to facing Dunning, with the full force of his rage directed at us.

We pounded down the steps, and as we neared the door that I thought connected to the room and balcony onto which Dunning had dropped, I shifted Lizzie to the inner wall, thinking I could at least place myself between her and the Count's wrath. We drew even with the door, continued around the spiral staircase. We would make it to the Great Hall without—

Jonathan Janz

With a bone-jarring thud, the door behind us slammed open.

I whirled and beheld Dunning, who leaned against the wall and glowered at me with inhuman rage. In his arms lolled the corpse of his beloved.

"You've set my castle ablaze," he said.

"You should have been consumed in the carpenter's house," I answered. "Your madness would have died with you."

"You'll never make it out alive."

"But we *are* alive," I said. "You died when Charlotte died. At least your humanity did."

His eyes flicked down to the object in my hand, but before he could comment, Lizzie yanked on my arm, and I had no choice but to race down the stairs after her. She was right. The time for reasonable discourse had long since passed. The castle was on fire. Dunning was bent on murdering us. Lizzie's family was held captive below, if they hadn't been slaughtered already. We hurried down the spiral staircase.

The tower room was ten stories above the Great Hall, yet we made it to the bottom with incredible speed. The knowledge that Dunning was hobbling after us had much to do with it, as did the fear of being incinerated in the growing conflagration. But most of all, I realized, we were driven by love. On Lizzie's part, love of her family. On mine, a burgeoning affection for this marvelous, steadfast woman, a woman whose reputation had been sullied by a vindictive charlatan.

I had to keep her safe. We sprinted toward the Great Hall.

When we burst inside, we were greeted with a sight that simultaneously horrified me and imbued me with hope. The hope stemmed from the knowledge that Lizzie's parents and little sister were alive. The horror arose at sight of three people strung up by their wrists and a throng of glitter-eyed fiends poking them with sharp objects.

Hubert, Juniper, and Violet Coyle were being tortured for sport. They dangled several feet off the ground, the ropes that

The Dismembered

bound them looped over chandeliers and affixed to iron wall hooks. The Coyles' garments were ripped to tatters, in several places revealing bloody flesh.

"The Count is defeated!" I thundered.

As one, the crowd turned toward me, and the instant they discovered what I held aloft, their expressions transformed from sadism to disbelief.

I brandished Broxton's severed head. "Your taxidermist is as lifeless as his subjects. McCray, Crawley, and Maximov have been killed. Your master lies bleeding to death in the tower, his life's work consumed by flames."

Miss Nichols, who'd moments before been shouting orders and brandishing a rapier, stepped forward. "You're lying."

I nodded toward the door. "The front courtyard affords a view of the tower. Why not see for yourself?"

No give at all in Nichols's face. "Bazemore," she said, "see to the tower."

The servant named Bazemore was a gangly youth of scarcely twenty years. He hastened to the enormous double doors leading out of the castle, and after some struggle, managed to prise them open.

Good, I thought. *One less thing to worry about.*

Bazemore hurried into the courtyard and gazed up at the tower.

"He's right, ma'am! The tower's lit!"

The pronouncement's effect was instantaneous. A full half of the crowd broke toward the stairs. We moved aside to let them pass. A good many of the servants sprinted toward other hallways, perhaps hoping to save their possessions before the castle went up in flames.

But Miss Nichols and her rapier remained fixed in place, barring us from Lizzie's captive loved ones. Three other servants, two young men and a red-haired woman, joined Nichols. Soon, Bazemore returned to the group.

Jonathan Janz

Miss Nichols grinned a singularly unpleasant grin. "Take him, Harrington."

And with a grin cold enough to freeze saltwater, one of the men pulled out a revolver and fired it at me.

Twenty

The first shot missed, but I knew our luck was stretched thin. For one, the Count was limping down the stairs behind us, and in moments, he'd encounter the crowd racing to his aid. Secondly, if Harrington's Webley revolver was properly loaded, he yet possessed five more shots.

I thrust the bone saw into Lizzie's hands. "The rope," I said.

She didn't hesitate. While Lizzie broke for the iron rings to which the ropes suspending her loved ones were tied, I dashed toward the gun-wielding Harrington, moving in a zigzag to minimize my chances of being killed by his revolver. He fired on me again and missed.

Four more, I thought. At the outset of my approach, fifty feet had spread between us. I had nearly halved that, and from such a close distance even the worst marksman would succeed in bringing down his quarry.

But Bazemore saved me. He pointed toward the iron hooks and shouted, "Miss Nichols, she's gonna cut 'em!"

Harrington glanced in that direction. My heart sank, sure he would shoot Lizzie. But Harrington handled the Webley like a child at play, and as I neared his position, he fired at Lizzie and missed.

Three shots left.

As I bore down upon Harrington, he took aim at Lizzie, raising the revolver to a proper shooting position this time.

I shouted, "Harrington!" and as he turned toward me, I hurled Broxton's head at him. The sight of the bloody head proved enough to shatter his concentration. He fired wildly, thrust both hands in the air, perhaps meaning to intercept the head before it crashed into him.

But my aim had been true. Broxton's head smashed into Harrington at chest level, knocking the gun from his hand and knocking him off his feet.

I went for the gun.

Another male servant, an able-bodied youth of perhaps eighteen, leapt for the revolver at the same moment. We hit the ground, both with a hand clenched on the Webley's hot surface. A sound from our left arrested our attention. The first rope had snapped, Lizzie and her bone saw having made short work of it. Violet dropped to the floor. She landed nimbly, and though her clothes were torn, the look on her face bespoke of grim mettle.

As Lizzie set to work sawing through the second rope, I wrested the revolver from the young servant's grip. The boy immediately grabbed for it, but I rolled away, pointed it at his face. "Don't make me do it," I said.

But I could see he cared little for threats. Maybe the Count's obsession had communicated itself to his servants. Maybe the boy believed he was as durable as his master. Whatever the case, he lunged for me, and with sorrow in my heart, I pulled the trigger. The slug slammed into him below the left eye, killing him instantly. The young man fell dead at Miss Nichols's feet.

Nichols looked up at me, her expression impassive. "Only one bullet to go."

She was right, of course. There were four servants present, two men and two women, and the Count would be arriving with the rest of the mob at any moment.

The Dismembered

"Mother!" Violet shouted.

I looked that way and saw Juniper tumble awkwardly to the floor. She grasped her ankle.

Miss Nichols glanced at the young male servant next to Bazemore. He had red hair and a thick upper body. "Cullen, stop the bitch," Nichols said.

The red-haired youth stalked toward Lizzie, who'd begun to saw through the final rope, and as the boy drew nearer, something in my mind clicked.

I leveled the revolver at the red-haired boy. "Don't move!"

Miss Nichols sucked in breath. "You can't shoot him!"

The boy had indeed frozen, but our time was almost at an end. I fancied I could hear voices behind me, the mob flowing down the stairs like a pestilence.

I nodded. "Tell your son to kneel on the ground and put his hands behind his head."

She shook her head, "You'll kill 'im! You'll put a bullet in his head!"

"Some of us," I said, "retain our humanity."

"Mom?" the red-haired boy said.

Nichols's mouth twisted, but she murmured, "Do as he says, Cullen."

The red-haired boy knelt and laced his hands behind his head.

The younger female servant flew at me. I'm ashamed to admit I hadn't given her much thought prior to her maniacal attack. Short, rail-thin, the young woman was no older than Cullen and so innocuous-seeming that I couldn't imagine her stepping on a spider, much less attempting to kill me. But attempt it she did.

Before I could react, her fingernails had torn swaths of flesh from my neck, the pain like a jug of icewater flung over my skin. Hissing, I thrust an elbow at her, struck her a sound blow in the shoulder, but in the next moment she was back at me, clawing and growling like one of Erskine's hounds. I didn't want to hurt her, and I knew I must preserve my final shot, so I did the only thing I could think to do. I brought the butt of the revolver down on her head. The sound curdled my blood, as did the sight of her boneless body toppling backward to the floor. Bazemore looked up at me, anger kindling in his young face. Maybe the female servant was his girlfriend.

I didn't care. He took a step in my direction, but I shook my head. "Don't," I said.

Bazemore froze. At that moment, Hubert Coyle dropped to the floor with surprising grace. Indeed, despite the score of wounds and the blood he'd lost, Lizzie's father looked more alive than he ever had.

Hubert smiled at me. "I'm glad you came to Altarbrook."

Under other circumstances, I would have been touched by the sentiment. As it was, I could think only of escape. "Can your wife make it?"

"Yes," came her immediate response.

"Arthur!" Lizzie shouted.

The strength drained from my legs. I knew what I'd find even before I saw the shadows of the servants dancing on the walls through the staircase doorway.

"Can we make it to the coach?" I asked Hubert.

He'd already taken his wife's hand and was hurrying toward the open front doors. "We have to," he said, "if we want to live."

Twenty-One

We left Bazemore, Miss Nichols, and her son Cullen behind. Though we hadn't yet glimpsed the tide of servants pursuing us, we heard their voices clearly enough. As the surviving members of the Coyle Family and I shambled through the courtyard toward the coach, I had no doubt that Dunning's lunatic disciples were already racing through the castle entryway to prevent our escape.

Hubert and his wife were at the fore of our group. "Can you drive?" he called to me over his shoulder.

"Yes," I answered.

"Have you ever driven a coach?" Hubert asked.

"Never," I said and sprinted toward the posts where our horses were tethered. Had I time I would have explained how much research I'd done about the animals for my writing.

But reading about horses was a far cry from actually riding them.

I reached the team a good thirty feet before the Coyles, so that by the time Lizzie began shepherding her sister and her parents into the carriage, I had already untethered the pair of lead horses from their posts. I knew I shouldn't risk a glance toward the castle, but I did anyway. At that moment a flood of servants surged through the doorway, but what gave me pause was the sight of Bazemore and Cullen Nichols dashing not in our direction, but toward the stables.

Were the boys going to pursue us on horseback? The thought filled me with dread. Previously, I had imagined us clattering away into the night, injured but alive, the nightmare of Castle Magnus behind us. Now I realized that was fancy.

I manipulated the reins and spoke to the horses the way my equestrian books suggested, and while the animals didn't heed my directions with much precision, they listened well enough to back away from their posts and set off at a steady canter toward the main road. Though the crowd was surcharged with lunatic passion, they were on foot and posed no threat to our speedy horses. Soon we were galloping at a brisk pace, the angry mob receding behind us. I wondered if Bazemore and Cullen Nichols had retrieved their horses yet, wondered whether Dunning himself would join the pursuit, but as we rounded a bend, I realized we were closer to deliverance than I had previously suspected. Though the passage through the mountains was narrow, our current position allowed a glimpse of the road below. I spotted the bridge, though it lay a goodly distance ahead. If we could cross the yawning gulf that separated Castle Magnus from the rest of the world, I believed we could yet survive.

I heard hoofbeats behind us.

I shot a look over my shoulder and felt my spirits plummet. Not only were Bazemore and Nichols pounding after us, they had retrieved two more horses from the stables with new riders. One of them I didn't recognize, a man of perhaps forty years with a wild mane of blond hair streaming out behind him.

The other was Count Dunning. His pant leg glistened. I had no doubt he'd fractured his leg in the fall, and even in my dire plight, I marveled at the man's tenacity.

I returned my attention to the road just in time. We were fast approaching a drastic curve, and our coach was racing toward it

The Dismembered

at a rate far too frenetic. I forgot all about my research on equestrianism and leaned away from the yawning abyss. The horses thundered around the bend, the coach swinging deliriously over the drop. I heard voices screaming from within the coach, the loudest of which belonged to Hubert Coyle. Unaccountably I found a smile touching my lips even before the coach bounced from two wheels down to four again.

When we straightened out, I shot a glance behind me and watched the four riders navigate the curve without difficulty. They were gaining.

Unconsciously, my hand went to my hip pocket, where I'd stored the revolver. I only had one shot left and four adversaries to defeat. My only hope was that their flight after us had been so precipitate that they'd not had time to arm themselves.

This question was answered in the next instant, for a rider—not Dunning—had drawn even with the bouncing carriage and set to attacking it with a rapier.

It was Cullen Nichols, the red-haired son of the cook.

A flurry of activity to my left revealed the presence of another rider. I glanced that way and spotted Bazemore drawing closer. He was groping with one wraithlike arm to gain a handhold on the side of the carriage. An arm shot out of the carriage window, and then Bazemore was veering away from us, shaking his hand in pain and spitting curses. I wasn't sure what had happened until a face appeared beside me, Lizzie having somehow climbed out the carriage window and maneuvered her way onto the box seat with me.

"Didn't like my fingernails," she muttered. "I'll drive. You deal with him."

At a glance I saw that Bazemore was swerving toward us, still intent on boarding the coach, still eager to risk his life on his master's orders.

It infuriated me, the manner in which Dunning had corrupted this youth and so many others. He'd led Sarah to her death, had nearly done the same to Violet. His magnetism, his thirst for knowledge, all his gifts were aimed toward vile ends, and I realized the only hope for us was to kill the Count himself, to slay this dragon and in doing so, render purposeless his followers. But first I had to deal with Bazemore, who was even now latching onto the side of the coach.

I handed Lizzie the reins as he climbed up, a gleaming dagger jutting from one hand. I clambered over the coach roof, but a look down at Bazemore, who was attempting to enter the coach window, revealed Violet holding something aloft, an object that caught the moonlight and glittered like polished onyx.

It was Jimmy Coyle's absinthe bottle.

Violet smashed the bottle over Bazemore's head. The young man squealed in pain and his grip on the coach window loosened. His feet skimmed along the rough mountain road. Violet thrust the jagged bottleneck at Bazemore's face and gored him in the cheek. This time he positively howled and, forgetting his situation, relinquished his hold on the windowsill. He was yanked under the rear of the coach, and my last glimpse of him revealed a belly ripped open by the unforgiving wheel, Bazemore's entrails spilling out as he tumbled after the coach. I looked away, sickened.

And gasped when another figure sprang onto the roof behind me.

The crazed zealot with the stringy blond hair. The man's eyes were huge and bloodshot, his teeth splotchy nubs. He reminded me of a pirate, though such a designation dishonored even that lowly profession. His shirt was open, revealing a chest crisscrossed with scars, not of the sort one would sustain in a fight, but rather in a symmetrical pattern suggestive of rituals and bloodletting. He advanced on me, a wicked-looking knife clutched in one hand. The blade was curved, the handle pale, as though fashioned from an elephant's tusk. One second we were staring at each other from opposite ends of the shuddering

The Dismembered

coach roof. The next, he was darting toward me, the curved blade whickering a centimeter from my nose.

The blond-haired man darted at me again, this time going for my legs. I glanced down, discovered a shallow slit in my thigh. Behind the blond assailant, Dunning and his black steed raced toward the carriage. Young Nichols had pulled up beside us, but at present did not attempt to board.

The blond man leapt at me. I ducked, the blade whooshing over my head, and drove a shoulder into his midsection. I seized him and whipped him onto the coach's roof.

But he didn't let go of the blade, instead drove it toward the side of my head. I snagged his wrist, redirected the blade toward his face. His bloodshot eyes became gaping moons, and just before the blade plunged into his forehead, he let go of the knife, which fell with a dull thud onto the roof. I longed to throttle him, but he was powerful and energized by his mad devotion to the Count. I couldn't risk a protracted hand-to-hand struggle. I grabbed for the knife. He anticipated me, attempted to parry my hand, but I was faster. My fingers closed on the handle. I lifted the knife, but grunted as he kneed me in the belly.

He pushed away from me, scrambled on hands and knees over the coach roof, evidently intending to attack Lizzie. If he harmed her or was somehow able to arrest the progress of the carriage, all would be lost. The bridge was fast approaching. Any sudden veering would send us plummeting off the edge toward the deadly rocks far below. In desperation, I flung myself at his back, thinking only to prevent him from harming Lizzie. It was providence that I led with the knife.

It punctured his ribs, his body arching in agony. He howled out his hurt, his arms upflung, and before he could recover, I shoved him sideways off the roof. He hit the road headfirst, the terrible crunching sound audible even above the clatter of the horses. His momentum carried him over the edge of the bridge, his broken body disappearing into the fathomless murk.

Jonathan Janz

The coach decelerated. I swung around to face Lizzie and felt my throat constrict. We had bested two of Dunning's men, and the Count himself had not yet reached the coach. But it didn't matter.

Cullen Nichols had made it to the driver's box.

He held a dagger to Lizzie's throat.

Twenty-Two

For several moments, I worried Lizzie would rebel against Nichols. Apparently, Nichols harbored similar concerns, for he pressed his dagger to the side of her neck with more force than necessary. "You'll make a pretty face for my master's lady," he murmured.

Lizzie winced. She had no choice but to haul back on the reins.

I glanced over my shoulder at Castle Dunning, where reddish flames licked the tallest tower and black smoke rose into the night. The castle wouldn't survive the night.

Neither, it seemed, would we.

In short order the carriage trundled to a stop. I knew I could make a move toward Nichols, but positioned as I was nearly a dozen feet from him, and with but a single shot in the revolver—a shot impeded by Lizzie's captive body—I knew my chances of killing Nichols while saving Lizzie were minuscule. I kept the gun stowed in my pocket.

As the Count's horse moved up beside the stopped coach, Nichols seemed to pick up on my thoughts. He said, "You stole Harrington's Webley. I'd like to have that back, if you'd be so kind."

"I lost it in our escape," I returned. "You'll find it in the courtyard."

"Sure I will," he answered. "Why don't we continue our talk on the road?"

"Don't listen to him," Lizzie said, then sucked in air when he increased the dagger's pressure. I had no choice but to comply. Descending the side of the coach was difficult, but Hubert surprised me by half-catching me before I fell.

"You're all so genteel," Dunning remarked. "But your simpering regard only hastens your undoing. Didn't I teach you anything, Violet?"

She gritted her teeth. "You taught me how basely a man can behave. To what depths he can sink."

Dunning merely smiled. He limped away from the coach, toward where Nichols stood with Lizzie held at knifepoint.

"You see," Dunning said, hands laced before him, "it is your morality that chains you." He gestured toward Lizzie. "You know you'll die by returning to the castle, yet return you will if I threaten to kill Miss Elizabeth. Your morality gives you no other option."

Hubert muttered, "The revolver."

I slipped it into his hand.

"You are all plagued with guilt," Dunning said. "You can't allow Elizabeth to die, not after consigning Sarah—"

A shot shattered the stillness of the bridge. Cullen Nichols's head snapped back, a gout of blood squirting from the center of his brow. His body slithered to the ground, leaving Lizzie six feet from Dunning.

No one moved. My mind implored Lizzie to run. I imagined encircling her with my arms and kissing her firmly on the lips as I carried her to safety. I imagined the look she would give me as our kiss ended.

But none of that happened. Instead of running, Lizzie went for Nichols's dagger.

She meant to kill Dunning herself.

Twenty-Three

"Lizzie!" I screamed, already sprinting toward her.

She never glanced at me, only lunged for the dagger, which had fallen a foot or so from where Nichols lay. Count Dunning, as savvy as he was, only stared at her a moment, as if the bridge itself had come alive and assaulted him with stone fists.

Lizzie reached the knife. Dunning dove at her. Lizzie jerked it up just as Dunning's body collided with hers. She toppled backward, Dunning's powerful frame knocking her off her feet. They landed on the hard stone, but it was Dunning who cried out the loudest. She'd stabbed him in the belly.

But Dunning still struggled.

"It's me you want, Dunning!" I screamed, sprinting toward them. "It's me!"

Their arms were a shifting tangle. I was nearly to them when Lizzie cried out. As I bore down on them, I saw why. Dunning had extricated the dagger from his stomach.

Only ten feet away, I bellowed in heartbreak as Dunning raised the dagger and whipped it across Lizzie's chest. Blood bubbled from an ugly crimson trench.

I leapt at Dunning.

Jonathan Janz

Who saw me coming and pivoted to thrust the dagger at me. I slammed into him, knocking him off Lizzie, but the blade impaled the crook of my arm, sending a fireblast of pain through my elbow.

Dunning and I rolled together, the Count digging the blade deeper. I cried out, but I knew if I detached myself from the Count, he would prevail. The throng of servants would be upon us soon, and though none of us were the equal of Dunning, I knew our only chance was to defeat the fiend now, before his legions joined the fray.

The blade sank deeper, skewering my elbow like a tender cut of meat. Despite the shrieking pain, I drove with my legs and aimed a shoulder at Dunning's throat. The gambit worked, the collision knocking Dunning onto his back, his iron grip finally broken from the dagger handle.

"Look out, Arthur!" Violet shouted. "The edge!"

I shot a look beyond Dunning's prostrate body and saw the precipitous drop from the bridge's edge. I envisioned the jagged shards of rock waiting below. No one, not even a demigod like Dunning, could survive such a fall.

I lurched toward Dunning, the dagger still buried in my arm. Though I kept my bleeding elbow tucked into my midsection, the pain that issued from it was enough to blur my eyes and muddle my brain.

Dunning coughed, a spatter of blood leaking out the corners of his mouth and staining his teeth red. He leered at me. "I enjoyed killing your father, Pearce."

In that moment, with his face outlined by the yawning abyss, it wasn't hard to imagine this monster luring my father to this hellish realm and slaughtering him in his quest to resuscitate Charlotte.

"Trusting others," I said through gritted teeth, "is not a flaw."

I grabbed hold of the Count's throat and squeezed. Dunning's corded neck writhed under my grip. Blood bubbled

The Dismembered

over his teeth. I stared into the Count's mad eyes and saw only hatred there. He reached up, grasped the handle of the knife jutting from my arm. Twisted.

Anguish like none I'd experienced howled through my elbow. I could feel the knife scraping bone, the sharp blade shredding sinew and gristle.

Dunning grinned.

With tears of pain in my eyes, I reared back, whipped my head down at Dunning's face. My forehead collided with his nose, the concussion driving Dunning's head into the stone of the bridge. The Count bellowed in agony as the blood gushed from his nostrils.

The sight of all that blood reminded me of my father, how Dunning had slaughtered an innocent man to further his insidious plot. I thrust a knee into Dunning's crotch. The Count doubled-up, and as he rocked onto his side, I shoved him with my good arm toward the bridge's edge. His upper body leaned out over the precipice, and realizing he was about to fall, his eyes shot wide. He seized me by the right hand, the hand I could no longer feel because of the ghastly damage done to that elbow.

I placed my good hand on Dunning's face and shoved it toward the brink. "My father," I said, "was worth a thousand of you."

I pushed with all my might. Dunning's shoulders and mid-section scraped over the edge of the bridge. He yelled something inarticulate, began to drop.

Then I was being dragged over the edge too, the Count's grip on my bleeding arm implacable. I stared down at Dunning, whose body dangled over the abyss. My gaze riveted onto his dark eyes. I realized he was laughing. My body slid forward, began to lean downward, my demise only inches away.

Hands fell on my legs. Voices behind me.

Hubert, Juniper, and Violet.

Another figure appeared in my periphery. I craned my head to see who it was, expecting the mad-eyed faces of Dunning's servants. Lizzie stared back at me. She grasped me around the waist, fought to pull me to safety.

Yet even with the combined force of the Coyles compelling me upward, the dual weight of Dunning's body and mine proved too great.

I was sliding toward my death.

"The knife," I grunted.

Though I could see Lizzie was fighting to remain conscious, I discerned strength there too, a singlemindedness that rivaled the Count's. She scooted forward to the edge of the bridge, so that her torso, like mine, hung over the edge. She grasped the knife handle protruding from my elbow, but paused, a pained look on her face.

"I won't be able to get at him," she said.

It was true. Dunning grasped my bleeding hand, and my arm was longer than Lizzie's. For her to slash the Count's fingers, she would have to be lowered by the ankles, and there was simply no way to accomplish that task. Even with Hubert, his wife, and Violet holding onto me for dear life, I was losing ground. Any moment I would plummet with the Count toward the lethal stone spires of the valley floor.

I shook my head. "I need you to cut *me*."

She glanced at my mangled elbow, and her eyes widened in dread.

"Arthur, I—"

"—have to," I finished. "You have to. It's the only way."

"She isn't strong enough," Dunning spat. "She doesn't have the guts."

Voices sounded behind us. Dunning's servants were approaching.

Grasping my wrist, Dunning began to haul himself upward.

The Dismembered

"Lizzie," I said, doing my best to hold her gaze. "Do this, and you'll deliver us."

With a moan, Lizzie hacked at the already ruined crook of my arm.

The pain was unspeakable.

Dunning bellowed, realizing that Lizzie was executing my gory plan. I cried out too. I realized I was weeping, but for once, I didn't care whether I appeared weak in front of someone else. I knew Lizzie wouldn't judge me. I closed my eyes and tried to prepare myself for the final stroke.

But when it came, it was the most hideous agony I'd ever experienced. I howled as my forearm tore loose of the elbow, the blood spraying over Dunning as he fell. His blood-splattered face twisted into a rictus of terror as he plummeted, his keening howl going on and on and seeming to gain in strength even as the darkness enveloped him, even as the crags of rock dealt his body the final killing blow.

I was hauled back from the edge of the bridge, Hubert and Juniper grasping my legs and Violet already fashioning a tourniquet to staunch the bleeding. I was on the brink of swooning, the pain and the blood loss finally conspiring to undo me. They rolled me onto my back. I felt a tugging and a pressure on my elbow. My body began to tingle pleasantly. I glimpsed the stygian sky and closed my eyes to rest.

I opened them when I heard the mob approaching.

Juniper was shaking me. "Get up, Arthur," she was saying. "We have to go."

Hubert and Juniper helped me up. Lizzie did what she could, but I could see the bloody trough spanning her chest and marveled that she remained on her feet.

She noticed my gaze and said, "The cut isn't that deep."

I glanced at her ruefully.

She shrugged. "I didn't say it felt good."

The Coyles helped me into the carriage.

"Who…," I began. "…who's going to—"

"Violet," Hubert said. "She's quite a rider."

I leaned against the seat. "Why didn't she drive us in the first place?"

Lizzie wrapped an arm over my shoulder. "Then you wouldn't have gotten the chance to play hero."

I laughed at that, but regretted it when the throb in my arm intensified.

The coach began to roll.

Hubert had leaned out the side window to gauge the distance of Dunning's mob, and what he saw evidently wasn't encouraging. He swatted the ceiling of the carriage. "Hurry, Violet! They're almost upon us!"

I didn't need to lean out the window to see he was right. I could hear the shouting voices as clearly as the hoofbeats of our horses.

I turned, my face very close to Lizzie's. "If we don't make it, I just want you to know—"

"We'll make it," Lizzie said.

She was right.

Twenty-Four

It was seven months later when the head butler at Altarbrook poked his head through the library doorway and said, "Excuse me, Mr. Pearce, but your visitor has arrived."

Beside me on the couch, Lizzie favored me with a quizzical look. "You didn't tell me you were expecting someone."

I cocked an eyebrow. "Must a husband tell his wife everything?"

Her return look was as feisty as mine. "Yes," she answered. "He must."

Laughing softly, I took her hand with my remaining one and led her into the parlor where our visitor stood scrutinizing one of the portraits. The painting of Charlotte Pearce, I realized with an internal start.

When he faced us, I felt Lizzie's body turn to stone. But I refused to relinquish my grip on her hand.

"What is he doing here?" she demanded.

Dennis Bridger's saturnine countenance changed on the instant. "Ah, Lizzie," he said, a smirk lifting a corner of his mouth. "I wondered what kind of man would settle for a creature like you." A nod at my missing forearm. "Now I understand."

Lizzie started toward him, but I tightened my grip on her hand. She shot me a fierce look, but I managed to stay her with my expression. Her eyes told me I had better possess a sound reason for preventing her from murdering Bridger.

I said to him, "I'm glad you made the journey."

His gaze drifted to the painting. "Your man told me it would be worth my while. Otherwise, I wouldn't have wasted my time in a home of such iniquity."

I kept my voice pleasant. "What are your demands?"

"Double the normal sum."

Lizzie tightened. I said, "That seems awfully steep."

Without taking his eyes off Charlotte Pearce's face, he said, "Unless you want all of London to know what a whore you married, you'll pay and pay gladly." He nodded at the painting. "I want this portrait too. Add it to my fee."

"Your *fee*," a gruff voice said from across the room, "will be added to your list of offenses."

Bridger whirled and discovered Detective John Martin with Violet Coyle at his side. "For a blackmailer," Detective Martin said, "you do leave a great many loose ends."

Acid dripped from Bridger's words as he muttered, "You've got nothing, else you'd have charged me by now."

"We *had* nothing," Martin corrected. He nodded at Violet. "Until she got involved."

"It's funny," Violet said, looking happier than I'd ever seen her. "When someone deceives you the way Richard Dunning did, you begin thinking about the way an evil mind functions."

Lizzie was glancing from face to face with a bewildered expression. "Could someone please—"

"I decided to do something useful," Violet said. She patted Detective Martin on the shoulder. "Since John here was so helpful in aiding the local constabulary—"

"I was only doing what any officer—"

The Dismembered

"Twenty-two of Dunning's followers arrested and a sizable cash settlement?" Violet said, her eyebrows raised. "I'd say you did a great deal."

Detective Martin waved her off, but I could tell he was pleased. And that pleased me. Martin was a good man and had been instrumental in transforming what might have been another nightmare into a masterclass of expedient justice.

"I'm getting out of here," Bridger said, and started toward the door.

Where Hubert and Juniper Coyle stepped through, barring his way. "You'll go nowhere but jail, Mr. Bridger," Hubert said. "For what you've done to Lizzie and a dozen other young women."

Bridger froze, his eyes bugging.

"I'm afraid that's not the worst," Detective Martin said, moving closer to Bridger. "We knew all about the blackmail schemes, but the nature of the crime makes witnesses reluctant to testify. It was something Miss Violet discovered that changed everything."

Bridger leveled a forefinger at Violet, but I noticed that his hand trembled. "She's as much a floozy as her sister! I've heard things about her and that Dunning—"

"Does 616 Feely Street ring a bell, Mr. Bridger?" Violet interrupted.

Bridger's color darkened to a deep mauve.

"I can see it does," Violet said. "The tenants there shared a highly interesting story with us."

Bridger licked his lips, looking suddenly like a caged animal. "You're not...you're no cop."

"She's better than a cop," Detective Martin said amiably. "She was able to interview the women you've been exploiting more effectively than we ever could have."

Bridger raised his chin. "I never made them do anything."

"We have proof," Martin said.

"And you're a bastard for coercing those young women into selling themselves," Hubert said.

"Two of them only thirteen years old," Juniper put in. "Mr. Bridger, how *can* you live with yourself?"

Bridger retreated a step. The portrait of Charlotte appeared to gaze down at him in judgment. "You rich sons of bitches. You've got no idea what it's like to scratch out a living."

"I know what it's like," I said, stepping forward. "And I know that doesn't give a man license to harm others. If anything, it should instruct him on the importance of protecting those in need."

Bridger glowered at me, teeth bared. "You deserve this whore. She's been with every man in London, and now she has to settle for a one-armed—"

I unleashed the most violent blow of my life, a barbaric uppercut that lifted Bridger off his feet and sent him sprawling on the floor.

Chuckling, Detective Martin hauled him to his feet. "Funniest thing about these old mansions," he said, handcuffing Bridger. "You never know when you're going to take a tumble down the stairs."

Before anyone could react, Lizzie flew at him and delivered a fist to the nose that, if anything, surpassed my own in violence.

Detective Martin caught Bridger before he fell and began dragging him toward the doorway. "I'll make a note to have that staircase fixed, Mr. Coyle. Don't want anyone else breaking his nose."

A trail of blood pattering the floor after him, Bridger was escorted out of the parlor, where a pair of Martin's men awaited.

In the silence that followed, Lizzie stared at her little sister. "Why did you do it?"

"For Father," Violet said at once. She appeared to soften. "And for you. For myself also, I suppose. To feel useful."

Lizzie smiled crookedly. "You're definitely useful."

Twenty-Five

After a satisfying lunch, Lizzie and I made our way through the forest behind Altarbrook, a blanket slung over my shoulder and a bottle of Cabernet in my hand.

"Do you suppose Violet will go for Mr. Martin?" Lizzie asked. "He certainly fancies her."

"Don't know," I answered. "She does enjoy his company."

It had rained that morning, and a warm mist cast a veil over the woods. Lizzie reached out, touched a rain-kissed leaf. "Do you suppose his ex-wife bothers her? Or his age?"

I shook my head. "Violet's not going to hold his past against him. After all, we all have one."

"No question of that."

"As for the age difference," I went on, "Violet is mature beyond her years. She has seen much of life for one so young."

"True," Lizzie allowed, "but what of Count Dunning? I can't imagine her first experience with an older man will work in Martin's favor."

Though she and I had spoken of Dunning on several occasions since that terrible night, the utterance of his name still effected a psychic chill in me. Frowning, I said, "Dunning was centuries older than Violet, not a mere decade like Martin."

Jonathan Janz

Lizzie sobered. "I'd forgotten."

We continued in companionable silence until we reached a fork in the path. I started to go left, but Lizzie reached out and took hold of the shortened sleeve of my missing forearm. The doctor had been able to stitch it decently enough, but I won't deny the truth: I missed the use of my right hand.

Perhaps sensing my veering toward melancholy, Lizzie gave my sleeve a little tug. "Thank you for clearing my name."

"It was Violet," I answered. "Violet and Detective Martin."

"As always, you downplay your own importance."

I began to protest, but Lizzie overrode me, "A year from now, you won't be able to go anywhere without readers accosting you."

I couldn't help but smile at her reference to *Scarlet*, my recently completed novel. "Just because a publisher paid me a handsome sum of money—"

"The book is worth a hundred times that," she said. "It will place you on par with Stoker and Shelley."

I'm afraid I blushed. Even after living with Lizzie for seven months, I hadn't grown accustomed to her adoration. "You honor me too much."

"Arthur," she said and waited for my eyes to reach hers. "You're the truest man I've ever met."

I couldn't help but smile.

She led me down a narrow trail. We walked in silence for a minute before reaching the graveyard. Here were numerous monuments, some of them centuries old. There was no doubt to whose graves we were going, the same graves we visited each week.

Charlotte Pearce's body had finally been interred in the soil of Altarbrook. In life she had loved Richard Dunning. And despite what the man had become, I had to admit a grudging respect for the manner in which he'd cared for her after the horror of the carpenter's burning house. But even had Dunning's

The Dismembered

body been recovered—a proposition made impossible by the treacherousness of the valley and the wolves that lurked in that shadowy domain—the Coyles could never have allowed his remains to join Charlotte's at Altarbrook. The acts he'd perpetrated, the murders of Jimmy and Sarah, the marrow-deep evil that had possessed him in the end, these truths forbade a reunion between him and his beloved.

Nevertheless, we did what we could for Charlotte.

Though unsure about religion, Lizzie led us in prayer at the graveside. As was our custom, we picked a few wildflowers and scattered them near the headstone. We moved on to Sarah's grave, then Jimmy's, uttering prayers and placing flowers by both. That done, we moved deeper into the forest. The day was warm enough to dry the moisture wrought by the morning showers, and as we reached our favorite spot, I noted how breezeless the clearing was, how intense the sun glare.

I nodded toward the far edge of the clearing, which was shadowed by oaks and sycamores. "Would you prefer the shade?"

She led me to the center of the clearing, where she spread the blanket and began unbuttoning the back of her sky-blue dress. "I've had enough of darkness," she said. "I want you to see me in the light."

I watched the front of her dress come loose, her chest-length scar revealed. Pale, gleaming, the place where she'd been slashed by Dunning spanned from one shoulder to the other. The dress loosened, and she let it fall. My eyes lowered to her breasts. The sight of them made my knees a bit wobbly, and perhaps catching the scope of my desire, Lizzie smiled and continued to liberate her body from her clothes.

Soon, she stood fully nude before me, the most glorious creature in the cosmos. So often in those first few months, I had felt self-conscious about my missing limb, but Lizzie's unwavering belief in me had reduced my apprehension.

"Now you," she said.

Jonathan Janz

I complied, and though it took me slightly longer to shed my clothing—buttons could sometimes be a chore—Lizzie watched me patiently, her eyes roving up and down my body, a combination of love and desire etched on her face.

When I had fully disrobed, we took a moment to stare at each other over the length of our blanket. What amazed me was the completeness of her abandon. There was inextinguishable ardor in her lovemaking, yet there was generosity too. A need to give pleasure as well as receive.

When I thought I could remain where I stood no longer, Lizzie finally came forward. I met her in the middle of the blanket, where we kissed deeply and hungrily. Soon we were sinking to our knees, and though Lizzie enjoyed lovemaking in all manner of positions, her preferred method was surprisingly traditional. I mounted her and continued to kiss her as her legs wrapped around me.

Some minutes later, we lay sated and beaded with perspiration. Far from filling us with discomfort, the glare of the sun soothed our flesh and bathed us in an exhilarating warmth.

Lizzie turned to me. "You realize if we continue this way, I shall soon find myself with child."

I met her frank stare. "How does that make you feel?"

"Excited," she said. "But unworthy."

"Unworthy is the last adjective I'd use. You saved me, Lizzie."

She pushed onto an elbow, leaned over me, and kissed me with an insistence that rendered me breathless. When our lips parted, she asked, "Can we remain at Altarbrook?"

"Certainly," I answered. "We'll need your parents to watch the child when we steal into the woods, won't we?"

She smiled. "I was thinking more because of the library. I want her to be a reader."

I raised my eyebrows. "Her?"

She kissed me again. "We'll have one of each."

The Dismembered

"That would require," I said between kisses, "a great deal of lovemaking."

She climbed atop me. "Something tells me you're equal to the task."

As we joined together once more, I smiled and kissed my incredible wife.

She was right, after all.

I was very much equal to the task.

About the Author

Jonathan Janz is the author of more than a dozen novels. He is represented for Film & TV by Ryan Lewis (executive producer of *Bird Box*). His work has been championed by authors like Josh Malerman, Caroline Kepnes, Stephen Graham Jones, Joe R. Lansdale, and Brian Keene. His ghost story *The Siren and the Specter* was selected as a Goodreads Choice nominee for Best Horror.

Additionally, his novels Children of the Dark and The Dark Game were chosen by Booklist and Library Journal as Top Ten Horror Books of the Year. He also teaches high school Film Literature, Creative Writing, and English. Jonathan's main interests are his wonderful wife and his three amazing children. You can sign up for his newsletter (http://jonathanjanz.us12. list-manage....), and you can follow him on Twitter, Instagram, Facebook, TikTok, Amazon, and Goodreads.

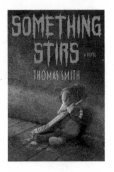